Written & Directed by Me, Mackenzie

A first novel by Elysia Nates

ISBN: 978-0-646-82754-4

Dedicated to my daughter, Ruby; my inspiration to ban the word 'said' and to be happy, every day. You are my inspiration to make life wonderful.

And to my Mum and Dad, Amanda, Renee and Stanley, for being the best family anyone could ever ask for. We are in our prime and love is forever.

"Shit, I'm sobering up. We need more drinkies."

Luke rummaged through the half-melted ice in the esky and pulled out a can of beer for himself and a Lemonade for me.

"Something non-alcoholic for you this time, Mack."

He rolled the can along the weathered surface of the trampoline and giggled quietly to himself. I caught the can as it approached my side and relished in the sweet "chhh" sound of its opening.

"Are you still laughing about that lame pirate joke?" I dared to ask.

"Because they AAAAARR!" Luke's laughter progressed to a silent wheeze as he repeatedly whispered his 'gold' punch line over and over again to himself.

"We're all feeling a little over the pirate, dude," I resigned with a laugh.

It was a Thursday evening in the glorious Adelaide summer. Cue music: Crowded House, Four Seasons in One Day, serenading us from the cd player propped up inside the open laundry window. My two best mates and I were eating Domino's pizza in the backyard of our house. It was mortgaged to my sister, Evie and I but Luke rented a room with us. It was a weathered red brick, semi-detached dwelling; rusted tin roof, eroding window frames, paint peeling off the ceilings, but it was home and it was a part of us all. Many a break up had been counselled behind that red brick exterior, many a drunken evening with someone losing their shit over Scattergories. Home and everything the word encompasses.

It was one of those evenings that just feeds your soul. It was around eight and the scorching hot summer day that peaked at forty-two degrees had finally cooled down to a bearable thirty-seven. In comparison, it felt like winter. There was an aura of peace and contentment all around us. The overgrown lawn sway gently in the warm breeze, the soothing sound of the crickets seductively crept into play and the rusted Hills Hoist in the middle of the yard waltzed with the sky as it dried the last two weeks of my underwear.

Oakley lay on the cool cement almost beneath us with his smorgasbord of garlic bread, Jim Beans and pizza with the lot. Luke and I were sprawled out on the trampoline with our abused pizza boxes and Cards Against Humanity rounds heaped to the side. It was an old school trampoline; no claustrophobic safety net around it or padding on the hinges, just a tattered, green, rectangular remnant of our dear childhood. When Mum put it out for the hard refuse collection after we bought this place, Evie and I snuck fifty dollars to the council truck driver to drop it off at our house instead. Mum is still determined to take it to the tip, five years later. I reckon Evie and I spent most of our childhood on this trampoline; reading Dolly magazines, acting out scenes from Grease and scripting conversations with our crushes that would never transition beyond the safety of the bouncing green surface. History. You can't throw out history, Mum.

So, we lay on our 1988 trampoline and gazed up at the hypnotising night sky. I was mesmerised by the seemingly miniscule stars and became instantly preoccupied with astronomical math and the philosophy of life. I may have been slightly inebriated at this point. To be honest, I had only had one Vodka Cruiser but it was enough to make me feel light-headed, most probably because it is only the second drink I have had in six years. I am not really allowed to drink alcohol but I'm in the mood to rebel against all that tonight.

I tried to deduce how many of me it would take to stretch between the Earth and the moon when a flash of lace caught my eye. I glanced over to the washing line and realised that my purple boy briefs and far less desirable white cotton comfies were on full display for the boys to see. It was as if the moon was deliberately being a bitch and smothered them with her luminescent glow just to make them that bit more obvious. My frame of mind quickly accelerated to an epic state of freaking out.

My internal panic attack was interrupted by Luke's swift and abrupt public declaration that he had regained composure and was ready to move on from the pirates.

"Okay kids, no more Aaaaars! Fuck me, it's hot! We got any more ice in the esky? Mack, how you can wear track suit pants on a day like this? I'm sweating my balls off!"

I reached through the hinges of the trampoline and rummaged through the esky underneath, past the cans of Coke and Guava Vodka Cruisers, to retrieve a handful of ice for Luke.

"My balls are tougher than yours. Are you going to eat that last bit of pizza?"

Luke slid his pizza box in my direction and ran the ice across his forehead. "Fuck you can eat a lot, Mack!"

I guiltily gazed around the surface of the trampoline. Crinkled Freddo wrappers and violated cheese Twisties packets were strewn about as if underwear thrown to the floor in a fit of passion.

Underwear. Shit. Piss off, moon!

"No, you're not fat," Luke quickly reassured me. I smiled at his genius.

"You know too much about women," I laughed.

"Hmmm, bet Oakley would disagree with you there, Mack."

Oakley remained engrossed in my copy of New Weekly. "Luke is hopeless," he replied ever so stoic.

"I can't even be insulted by that, it's the truth," Luke resigned.

Oakley was laying on his tummy, resting his head on his folded arms. I mentally recorded the image; his old, baggy jeans hung low on his back and his plain grey t-shirt cuffed at his shoulders. He looked like a 1950s rebel.

I glanced over to Luke, who was pre-occupied in his drunken state with grouping our pegs into colours, so I indulged in the opportunity to bask in the wonder that was Oakley Bains.

Definitely calls for a slow-motion scene.

Cue music: Tina Arena, I Need Your Body.

My eyes immediately fixated on his defined arms and slowly slid up to his perpetually rosy lips. His pale blue eyes were vivid in the evening dusk and his shaggy dark blonde hair glowed with the light of the moon, the strands almost ginger in the radiance. He was always in need of a haircut and could just about tie it into a pony tail now. I smiled as I imagined how sexy that would look on him.

Just as I was on the cusp of envisaging my fingers sliding down his torso, my eyes locked with Oakley's. I ceased breathing immediately. Shit. Shitty shit. My eyes widened in terror and I aggressively began to study my finger nails as if I had of course been doing that all along.

"Hate to bring it up," Luke thankfully spoke, "but what time is the appointment tomorrow?"

Shit. Oakley was still looking at me. He sat up and rested his arms loosely over his knees.

I exhaled my first breath in what felt like minutes. "One fifteen."

"Ooh she plays it so cool!" Luke joked. "We all know you're shitting yourself!" He winked and smiled at the same time.

Before I could think of a witty reply, Oakley waved the crinkled magazine in the air. "Bugger! Finished. Man, I wish New Weekly came out twice a week."

Luke and I glanced at each other with the same look of bewilderment on our face.

"No one stays in the closest these days, mate," Luke laughed. "It's perfectly acceptable to be gay."

"Do you really want to compare tallies?"

"Tallies?" I moaned, appalled on behalf of women everywhere. "Please tell me you are not referring to women as tallies?"

Oakley's smirk reined victorious. "The tally speaks for itself. Luke knows. Bow down to the King of the Tallies!"

Luke stood up on the trampoline and uncoiled his hand as he bowed his torso in the most theatrical of ways.

I rolled my eyes and shoved in another mouthful of pizza to drown out their juvenile sexism. "You guys are gross!"

"Says the chick talking with a face full of another man's pizza!" Oakley retaliated. His ridiculously gorgeous eyes rendered me a giggling mess.

"Keep it in your mouth, Mack, gross girl!" he drunkenly laughed.

"So, Miss Mackenzie, what time does my goddess fly in tomorrow?" I was surprised it had taken Luke this long to ask.

My sister, Evie, moved to Sydney six months ago for a two-year work contract and the three of us have been pining for her ever since. We have been doing Sunday Skype Nights but there has been a definite absence in our daily lives. My last appointment a couple of weeks ago didn't go so great; "Possibly twelve months, I'm so sorry to say," the good old doctor said. Evie pulled every string she could to transfer back to Adelaide. It has been rough without her and her infinite supply of optimism pushing us all through life.

"Just before twelve. We're going straight to my appointment from the airport so won't be home til threeish."

"AM?!" Luke panicked.

"No, dude," I stared blankly at him. "God, you freak out when you're toasted!"

"Toasted!" Oakley blurted out at the top of his voice. "Oh my god! Mack, remember that time at Solli's when you burnt the toast? Shit man, I haven't thought about that in years! Funniest shit ever! 'Quick, pour water on it!'"

And with this final mocking, Oakley well and truly lost it. He laughed so hard the dog next door began to howl in sync.

Nine years ago, I was working as a waitress at a trendy Melbourne Street restaurant, Solli's. I had just finished my Nursing Degree and was waiting for my registration to come through. The cook was a bit of a flirt, always complimenting the females who worked there and collecting hearts. He swaggered around the kitchen like James Dean. He was a suburban movie star; void of fame but in abundance of the looks that generally spawned it. His name was Oakley.

I was super shy and awkward back then. I was pretty sick as a teenager so never really learned the art of mingling or making friends. While the other kids in my year level were out on their first dates, I was hoping my hair would grow back in time for graduation.

We never spoke to each other but every Wednesday Oakley would steal the New Weekly magazine poking out of my black handbag decorated with Molly Ringwald badges. He would return it just as it was after his lunch break, only with a few editorial changes. He seemed to have a thing for Kim Kardashian and wrote things like "She loves me" next to her photo. My eyes popped out of my head when I checked out his usual commentaries a few days before the-soon-to-be-explained toast fiasco: next to a photo of Taylor Swift, he wrote, "you look like her, only prettier." I cut it out and still carry it in my purse to this day.

We were short staffed one Saturday morning during the breakfast rush so the manager, Gary, sent me to assist in the kitchen. Oakley was cooking the bacon and eggs orders. I heard one of the other girls, Edwina, bitch to herself "what a waste." It was true, I wasn't exactly confident enough to use the time in the kitchen like the rest of the girls would. I had never been able to mutter an entire sentence around him, let alone to him. But I still felt like I had won the lottery, and Edwina knew it.

It was cold so I moved the toaster to the bench space next to the oven. I popped on four slices of bread and read Edwina's scribbles about vegemite and no butter. Oakley looked smugly at the cardigan I was wearing, came over from his side of the bench, opened the door of the oven and said, "Put your hands in, you'll be warm in no time." His voice threatened Ryan Gosling for the title of Most Seducing Ever.

I smiled and roasted my hands at the door of the oven.

"Stick them in a bit, Mack, trust me."

I was simultaneously overjoyed that he knew my name and had assigned his own nickname to me, and pissed off with the universe for not allowing rewinds so I could hear it from his lips again and again. He stood right next to me, mere centimetres between us, bent his knees and stretched his arms out in the oven, roasting them as if in front of a naked fire. I looked at his hands for a little too long. I liked his hands. He had good hands. They deserve a close-up.

Then he smiled at me. Not just a normal smile, but a smile for me. Completely directed at me. Given to me and me alone. I felt ridiculously giddy on the inside. On the outside I probably looked like I was about to vomit.

He returned to his side of the island bench and commenced cutting slices of ham from the slicer. He moved his head along to an Eminem song on the radio. I was bummed about his taste in music but too mesmerised by his hands and the curvature of his torso as he lifted his shoulder with each cut to really care.

Like I said, I popped four pieces of toast on…

I worked at Solli's for four months before my shy and quiet demeanour evidently clashed with the hectic pace and the city folk's rushed lunchtime schedule. The toast seemed to be my final hurrah.

Gary pulled me aside the next week when he got the bill from the Fire Brigade.

"Look Mackenzie, it's not working out. None of the customers can hear a bloody thing you say. Plus, now I owe six hundred dollars to the bloody Fire Brigade. I'm sorry, I'm going to have to let you go."

"The toast just set off the alarm. Nothing actually burned down," I quietly justified to myself, out loud.

Gary raised his eyebrows.

Cue music: Oasis, Champagne Supernova. An intense heat erupted over my face; the capillaries under my cheeks began to burn and bring a scarlet blush to the surface. I could no longer hear the clanging of dishes or the ding of the cash register or the customers shouting that they have been waiting ten minutes to order and they only have forty-five minutes for lunch. The only sound that echoed around the café was that of my heart, pumping so fast it took the breath right from inside me.

We were next to a table with three stereotypically gorgeous women. They wore little Victoria Beckham style dresses and sipped on their tiny little lattes. One of them giggled, "we got the entertainment table."

I had never been fired before.

The deviant voice of Noel Gallagher echoed in my head and numbed the humiliation. I picked up my bag from underneath the sandwich bar and walked towards the exit of Solli's with my head held low. Past Edwina as she sniggered "totes brutal" to one of the other girls. Past the customers moving their fork around their plate to make it look like they were eating and not gawking at my disgrace. The door was a whole postcode away and my feet were encased in cement.

Finally, finally, the door handle was within my reach. I longed to hear its rusted turn as it released me from this moment.

I grasped it as if reaching out to the hand of God. I could feel the oxygen returning to my body. The handle turned in slow motion and the bell above dinged, almost mockingly.

I felt a hand rest on my shoulder and then reach over me to hold the door open.

Another hand rested on my lower back and guided me through the door, and I heard a whisper in my ear, "Don't look down, Molly girl." I turned my head to see Oakley standing between me and Solli's, shielding me from the humiliation. Tears cascaded my flushed cheeks, yet he made me smile despite it all.

"Bye, Oakley." I wondered if it meant the same to him that I knew his name.

I walked faster than my legs could carry me until I was safe behind my own walls.

Now that we would no longer be working together, I would never see him again. I slumped on the couch with a tub of white Magnum. Fucking depressing losing someone you never actually had.

But two days later, at the start of the weekend, Oakley showed up at my door with a block of Top Deck and Pretty in Pink on DVD.

"I thought you could do with getting your Molly on," he smirked as I stood, stunned, next to the opened door. "Plus, I haven't read New Weekly this week."

He stepped into my home as if stepping into my life, found his way to the couch, grabbed the remote, and became my best friend that very instant.

So that's the story of me and Oakley. I was obsessed with him, and he was too much of a man to buy his own copy of New Weekly.

As for the remaining member of our little clique, Luke; Evie had been friends with him since high school. Evie was never really interested in dating so when her Year 11 formal came up, she had to get set up with a boy from our brother school, Black Friars. His name was Luke.

She was true to herself and barely spoke a word to him. When K-Ci and Jo-Jo made the dance floor the place to be for romance with All My Life, Luke finally worked up the nerve to ask Evie to dance. Considering he had sat next to her all night and she hadn't even acknowledged him, he was either brave or oblivious. Evie scrunched up her face and simply responded, "good God, no."

As all the couples awkwardly pretended to know how to slow dance, Luke persisted and asked Evie for her phone number. His determination despite constant rejection impressed Evie, so she wrote down her number on a napkin, telling him, "I don't like talking on the phone." He called every Sunday for two months, after which Mum finally told Evie, "You will go out with that boy so you can let him down gently. I did not raise a bitch."

On their fourth date at the movies, Evie told Luke that she wasn't interested in having a boyfriend but was happy to continue being friends.

"Do you know what he said when I told him that?" Evie debriefed me as we lay on the trampoline that evening.

"I'll just have to be your best friend then. I just want to be around you." She smiled from ear to ear despite herself. "He's a bit silly, that boy."

They have had a couple of drunken flirtations here and there over the years but the underlying mateship between those two is insanely real. He idolises her and she him. Best friends in the truest meaning of it.

Now back to the evening at hand.

I lay on my back, staring up into the magnificent night sky. It was perfectly black. A huge black canvas sprinkled with glistening stars.

Oakley climbed up onto the trampoline and lay in the middle between Luke and I. I felt the weight of his body shift my own and I forgot to take a breath.

"Do you want me to come with you tomorrow, Mack?" he nervously enquired.

Cue music: Coldplay, Fix You. Very unlike me to feature a bit of Coldplay in the soundtrack of my life but sometimes life is its own DJ.

I pressed my lips firmly together, as if trapping my words from escaping. "I don't want to come with me tomorrow."

"I know, girl."

"It'll be okay, hey?" I searched his face for reassurance.

"You know it, Mack," his voice croaked.

I half smiled and looked back up at the sky. "Aren't the stars amazing? Like jewels on black velvet."

"Oh, fuck she's a poet now!" Luke laughed. "Quick, get this girl another drink!"

"Hey, Mack?" Oakley smirked.

"Yeah?"
"Nice undies."
Shit.

The Second Chapter

My mind slowly drifted into consciousness as the alarm sounded at seven the next morning. I lay in bed and refused to open my eyes. The lead taste in my mouth was so strong I wondered if I had been sucking on batteries over night without my knowing. My stomach was queasy. My skin was itchy. My head felt too heavy for my neck to support. Every inch of my body is being worshipped and rejuvenated by my blankets so the day can just fuck right off.

Stay in bed, Mack. Keep your eyes closed. The day can happen without you.

I gave in and let myself cry into my pillow. I was sick of waking up feeling like this.

My alarm had been sounding for exactly thirty-six seconds. I know this because Jordon just promised that he would never leave my side. New Kids on the Block were about to assure me that I would always be their Cover Girl, and the horrible feeling in the pit of my stomach began to subside with their melody.

I sat on the edge of my bed, the anxiety and nausea slowly leaving my body. I smiled and surrendered myself to the music. I allowed the air to escape deep from my lungs and inhaled as if trying to capture every molecule of oxygen in the room. I smiled as my boys sang my favourite line and I physically felt life return to my body. My shoulders grooved to the sweet beat and for a moment in time everything was perfect.

The chorus sounded and I leapt into the middle of the room in my oversized flannelette pjs, my heart and soul belting out the lyrics. I gave it everything I had, truly the performance of a lifetime. I could feel my body pleading with me to sit down; she was tired. For the next two hundred and twelve seconds, I needed her to just shut the fuck up and dance. Cancer holds my body hostage. New Kids on the Block paid the ransom and freed me. Sometimes, you just have to forget about life for three minutes, and sing the hell out of your favourite song.

By the time my alarm ended, I felt capable, in control and ready. I headed for my bedroom door and reached for my white knitted beanie, hooked on the door handle so I would never forget it. I slipped it on my head and made my way out to the kitchen.

Luke was standing in front of the window making coffee, dressed in a very smart grey suit, looking well prepared to be an adult for the duration of the working day.

Our dining table sat in the kitchen; it was one of those retro corner booths reminiscent of a 1950s Milk Bar. I bought it off Gumtree and may have loved it more than I love most people. I slid onto the bench seat and watched Luke as he put his dishes into the sink.

"So, are you going to ground me for playing my boys too loudly first thing in the morning?"

"Normally, yes. Particularly cos I've got a hangover. But today, no."

He placed a tall glass in front of me and winked.

"Not today, Mack."

My bottom lip dropped and my eyes welled with tears at the sight of the home-made chocolate milkshake before me.

"Thank you! I was secretly hoping for one of your creations today!"

The glass was filled to the brim and the smell of chocolate lingered around the entire kitchen. He had even decorated the whipped cream with flake sprinkles and Twirl sticks. To be honest, he makes me a special milkshake almost weekly, but it always blows me away. I never take it or him for granted. It always feels magical and unexpected, even though he makes me fifty-two odd milkshakes a year. I catch myself being so grateful to have a friend like him every single time he places the glass in front of me.

"Who counts calories on a day like today, hey? Besides, you could do with gaining twenty or thirty kilos!" Luke chuckled.

He slid onto the bench and looked down into his lap sorrowfully.

"And I'm really sorry I probably won't be here when you get home. I'm in court at three and I think it will be a late one for me. Call the second you finish the appointment, okay?"

His voice was breaking. "Promise?"

He was desperate and it broke my heart.

"I promise, Luke."

"Thank you." He drummed his hands on the table, signalling his preference to end that particular topic of conversation.

"Okay, I gotta get going now. Oaks will be here around eleven to drive you to the airport to pick up my goddess. I changed my sheets this morning if she wants to sleep in my room tonight."

"I'm pretty sure she'll be fine in her old room," I smiled back.

"I'm not fussed, I can shack up in her room. Bye, Mack," he whispered, gently kissing my forehead. "See you around nine tonight. I will totally wake you up if you are asleep so you may as well just wait up for me."

He grabbed his Crows cooler bag from the table and headed out the door. I looked down at the creation he had left me and began to blow my calorie quotient for the week. If I still bothered to have one. It was simply divine.

After "breakfast," I put on an old favourite, Alanis Morrisette's Jagged Little Pill and turned it up loud. Female angst resonated throughout the whole house. I set up my stool in the shower and screamed, not sang, along with the great Alanis.

After what felt like an excessively long time under the water, I dragged myself out of the shower and into my bedroom to get dressed. I sat at my dressing table with my pink Ikea towel wrapped around my body like a sarong and began to rub moisturiser into my arms and neck.

I looked at myself in the mirror and sighed at the sight. My neck was bruised and discoloured. My arms were weak and bony. My eyebrows were patchy, my eyes sunken. If I felt the way my body looked, I would surely be dead.

Just as clinical, environmental, psychotic, chronic, manic and any other type of depression that exists began to kick in, Alanis started singing about rain on a wedding day and I realised that my shower had almost taken up the whole CD.

"Ironic already? God, how long was I in the shower for?" I said to myself.

"Forty-five minutes," a voice came up behind me.

I jumped as the image of Oakley approached me in the mirror.

"Good morning, beautiful," he smiled.

I laughed and turned to face him.

"Beautiful was not the sort of adjective going through my head just now."

As I stood up, Oakley reached for my hands and pulled me in towards him, wrapping my arms around his waist. I giggled like a child.

"You are beautiful, Mackenzie."

I felt completely self-conscious and awkward and silly. I smiled at his shoes and bellowed a line from the song.

"Oh Christ, that's it! I'll be on the couch watching telly until you're ready to leave," he resigned happily as he left me to it.

I laughed as I watched him gently close the door behind him. I mentally replayed the moment where he pulled me close, editing my lines and rescripting myself as a much cooler, confident woman. The scene went through at least six different endings while I put on my make-up and got dressed in my faithful trackies.

I picked up my beanie from where I had flung it onto my bed after my shower and stopped in horror, realising that I wasn't wearing it when Oakley was in my room. The whole time. I pulled it on tightly and felt sick to my stomach. No one had ever seen me without it. Not even Evie.

"Are you watching Golden Girls?" I dared to ask as I made my way out to the lounge room.

"Blanche makes my list."

I rolled my eyes. "Everybody makes your list!"

"I object to that," he retaliated as he switched off the tv and peeled himself away from the couch. "Ready to go? I don't start work to 4, dinner shift for me today so we can take Evie out to lunch when we get her if you like."

"I've got my appointment pretty much straight after," I said softly.

"I know, but I prefer to live as if none of that exists."

He stroked my cheek with his perpetually warm hand and locked eyes with me. I smiled awkwardly and said, "time to go."

A look that could be described as disappointment brushed his face. "Okay, let's go get your sister. Luke will kill me if he finds out we made her wait."

We drove to the airport in silence. I put one of my mix CDs on and he didn't even pay me out when The Teen Queens came on. He just drove, and really concentrated as he did.

When we got to the airport Oakley told me he wasn't coming in but would park the car and wait for us. I asked if he was okay. He smiled and just said "always."

I got out of the car and walked into the airport. Oakley honked twice and drove off to find a park. Was he embarrassed because he saw my head? All bald and cancery? I hated myself for forgetting my beanie. I shouldn't have let him see me like that. What kind of friend thrusts their doom in your face like that?

I walked through the doors of the airport, apologising to Oakley over and over again in my head. I read the gate signs and channelled my attention into my mission; to find my sister and never let her go again.

The airport looked as if the whole of South Australia had squeezed itself through the doors. It was impossible to take a step without brushing shoulders with a stranger, or worse still, being bumped into. Every brush and every bump made me quiver with pain. I was being beaten up just by walking.

Then there were the stares. I usually get them from women. Everyone is so frantic going about their business; trying not to take their eyes off their kids amongst the herd, rushing to meet their boarding time, swearing at the automatic check-in station. But throw a person with cancer in the crowd, and suddenly everyone has all the time in the world to stare.

Two women stood near me at the baggage collection, I guessed waiting for their Loui Vuitton knock-off suitcases.

"Why wouldn't she wear a wig?" the pretty one asked the gorgeous one.

"If I had cancer, I would get a wig down to my waist, take the opportunity to get celebrity hair!"

They both chuckled and started compiling a list of fashion designers that could "really profit from branching out to head scarves." I kept my eyes fixated on the Arrivals door.

The thing about cancer is, it is ugly. I wish I could tell the pretty one that wigs made my head bleed. I wish I could tell the gorgeous one that by my fourth round of chemotherapy, my skin became so fragile that I would get skin tears just by having a shower. Back in high school when I first got sick, my head was covered in scabs and dry patches and the wigs aggravated my skin. I tried bandanas but my arms were too weak to tie them properly. I found my white beanie in an op shop. If I'd known I would end up needing it a second time around, I may have put a bit more thought into it and picked something a bit more stylish. Now I am scared to wear anything else.

But then the world got better. Cue music: The Bangles, Be With You. Evie came bundling through the Arrivals gate and burst back into my life. The song played loud as the world around me was reduced to a blur.

Evie stood outside the Arrivals gate, a swarm of annoyed people frantically moving past her, not that Evie was the sort of person who would care. She never minded if someone disliked her. She was unapologetically herself in everything she did in life. She was confident without being arrogant. She was brave without being overpowering. Her presence commanded an air of envy and admiration.

Her hair was longer, almost down to her shoulders now, and she was letting her naturally dark blonde hair grow through the packet platinum blonde she had been reliant on for the past few years. She wore denim shorts that I'm pretty sure a fourteen-year old would fit into and a slack fitting t-shirt that read 'Unicorns make me happy.'

She studied me as if looking at an old photo she found in a drawer. Her big blue eyes took in my image as her smile knocked off Julia Roberts for Most Joyous Ever. She took a few slow steps towards me and then charged with all her might, scooping me up into her arms like a gentleman carrying his bride over the threshold. The world returned to its regular pace and The Bangles faded out. We both laughed as if experiencing the sensation of laughter for the first time. Evie squealed "Mackie! Evie and Mackie in da house!" It was the best moment ever and I blatantly ignored my body's pleas of exhaustion.

She gently lowered my legs back onto the ground with the same speed and care she would use when removing the bottom brick in a game of Jenga. She held my hand and said "let's get the fuck out of here and have a great life, hey?" My bottom lip quivered and I nodded my head vigorously.

Evie grabbed her four duffle bags off the conveyer belt and we made our way to the exit, passing the pretty one and the gorgeous one who had been stalking our every move.

"Thanks for the stares," Evie spoke directly to them as we made our way past, "I find myself staring at beautiful things, too. Have a great day, and I'm sorry that no one ever stares at you."

I didn't look at their reaction, I just held onto my sister tightly and prayed that self-worth was capable of hopping from one body to the other.

Back at the car, Oakley was leaning against the boot with his arms folded, his usual pose. I contemplated taking out my phone to take his photo but thought he'd probably notice that. Plus, in twelve months, I doubt a photo would make a difference to me.

His face lit up and he ran towards us. I stepped away from my sister and he collided with her with the force of a semi-trailer slamming into a traffic light. They were both laughing and jumping up and down and hugging and loving the moment. I smiled and envied their energy. I could still feel the indent of Evie's fingers on my arms and legs.

Oakley drove us to Mum and Dad's house ahead of the appointment. We made it just in time. As we pulled up, Dad was getting in the car to drive off to his next customer. He beamed as he saw us and came rushing over to greet us.

Dad had been wearing the same style of glasses for as long as I can remember. They must have been from 1989 but they didn't look out of place; they looked like him. He was bald on the top of this head but his sides were meticulous and shone with a metallic glaze. It was 38 degrees today and he was still wearing his three-piece suit.

He embraced Evie and I in the same hug. I could feel myself sinking into him. My head rested on his chest and I breathed in his scent; Old Spice. He felt like home. I heard The Beatles in my head whenever I was around him.

"My girls," he chuckled, "my girls."

Mum came running out of the house, dressed in her nicest outfit I noticed and wrapped her arms around Dad and so too us.

"Let's get this done now, then off to tea tomorrow night!" Mum cheerily announced.

We waved goodbye to Dad and transferred the bags from Oakley's car to Mum's. Mum gave Oakley a quick hug and a "hello, dear, how are you?" before getting in the car without waiting for his response. Evie jumped in the front seat and I said goodbye to Oakley.

"What time does your dinner shift finish?"

"Ten, but I'll call you in my break, yeah?"

"Yeah", I replied, exhaling deeply. "Um, are you okay? Are we okay?"

Oakley sort of half-smiled and emulated my deep exhale. "I'm always okay, Mack. We're always okay. We do 'okay' pretty good."

He placed his hand over my collar bone and I returned his gaze awkwardly.

"Talk soon," he said and then walked off to his car in the street.

I watched him walk away and repeated his words in my head. We're always okay. We do 'okay' pretty good. Was the emphasis on 'always' or 'okay' or did I miss the point entirely?

"Get your butt in the car!" Evie called out, sticking her whole torso out of the window of the front passenger seat.

"Coming," I called out quietly and waved like Forrest Gump as Oakley drove off. He honked twice and seemed to laugh to himself as he drove past.

The drive to my appointment was wonderful and I never wanted to reach our destination. Cue music: Cool Rider from Grease 2. We cranked it up loud and Mum boogied her shoulders whilst continuing to smile at people who beeped at her for driving 47 kilometres per hour. We sang it to the heavens, every line in perfect unison. We were loud and crazy. Evie was taking selfies of us from the front seat. We pulled into the car park and Mum didn't turn the car off until the song had finished.

The building was architecturally amazing. White marble floors catching walls reminiscent of an old barn. Wooden beams stretched across the majestically high ceiling. Such a waste to use a beautiful building like this to tell people how many months they have left to live.

I was tired from all the walking I had done today so sat myself straight down in the waiting room. Mum went up to the lady behind the counter and informed her, "Mackenzie Dair, here for Doctor Young," in an intimidating tone that signalled she would make a scene if we had to wait an hour and a half like last time.

"Want a magazine?" Evie asked as she sat down next to me.

My head was bowed and I shook it gently. I just wanted to lay down and go to sleep. It felt like it was midnight. I wanted to vomit and then nap for ten hours.

Mum asked Evie a barrage of questions about her flight home and if everything was all settled back in Sydney. Evie said the company were going to sort out her unit as it was a company rental. Mum kept saying how happy Dad was to have all his girls home again. I tried to focus on their voices but they were getting further away until eventually I was sure they were in another room. I closed my eyes.

"Mackenzie, time to go in." Mum gently lifted my head and helped me stand to my feet. "Okay?"

She stood in front of me, protecting me, while I suppressed the nausea and readied myself to walk.

The three of us walked into Doctor Young's office holding hands. We sat in front of her obscenely wide desk like primary school children and awaited our discipline.

Doctor Young was lovely. I had been her patient since the beginning. I was 14 when I was first introduced to this world. I had treatment for two years before going into remission. I still finished high school on time and did my nursing degree but within three years of working as an RN, it came back. This is year six.

I had guessed Doctor Young to be about forty-five. She was an attractive woman and I imagined her changing into active wear at the end of the day to go to the gym straight from work. I guessed that she was married but didn't picture her with children. She most likely lived in Unley or North Adelaide. She would have watched shows like House, and Sherlock. I watched The Bachelor. She was actually a really nice person but I hated her so much I could barely pretend that I didn't. I don't even understand why.

Mum and Evie listened intensely. My eyes felt so heavy I wished a Minion would come and hold them open for me. My head kept bopping down and Doctor Young's words came in waves. "Possibly less time than we thought." "Completely stopped responding to the chemo now." "We can make her comfortable and explore other options."

When I woke up, I was laying in the backseat of Mum's car. Mum was driving, seemingly slower than her usual slow, and Evie was talking on the phone in the front seat. It sounded like Dad on the other end. I closed my eyes again and let sleep win.

The Third Chapter

I woke up in my bed, totally oblivious to the time or date. I had no idea how long I had been asleep for. I felt pretty good actually. A little bit nauseous, but awake. I felt awake.

I put my dressing gown and beanie on and left my room to search for signs of life.

Evie, Luke and Oakley were sitting out the back with Roxette's Greatest Hits playing through the laundry window. The Big L was on and I felt a surge of confidence, as if the universe had finally given me my own damn slow-motion scene.

Our wooden patio picnic table was decked out as if ready for a photo on an Instagram Food Lovers page. My eyes feasted on a buffet of fruit, cereal in canisters, pancakes, jugs of juice and even a stack of bread pinned down by some sort of skewer next to the toaster, connected by an extension cord running into the house. Oakley did like to cater when there was an occasion and Evie coming home was no doubt the highlight of our year.

The breakfast told me it was the morning. I was relieved but started praying that it was the morning straight after my appointment, and that I hadn't slept away three of the allotted days I had left.

Evie sat at the table wearing a strapless Hawaiian style dress. It was fluorescent green with ridiculously large and obnoxious-looking pink pineapples scattered all over it. It would look absurd if a normal person wore it in every-day life. Evie, however, was not normal. She could step out in a Pikachu onesie and still look like a supermodel on her day off.

Luke had his arm draped around Evie's shoulders and was in his traditional weekend attire; tailored shorts and a linen shirt cuffed at the sleeves. He made an effort with his appearance. I'm pretty sure he moisturised.

And then there was Oakley. As usual, sitting on the cement. As usual, looking like a movie star from another era. He had a perpetually unsure look on his face, as if he was forever pondering something. He could be grocery shopping, watching a movie, driving his car; he always looked pensive.

His hair was different today. It wasn't falling onto his forehead like usual; it was almost quiffed and perfectly styled against the shape of his head at the back. He was wearing his faded jeans that I love and a white t-shirt with the Degrassi High logo on it. I made him watch the entire Degrassi Junior High and Degrassi High series with me when I first found them on DVD about five years ago, plus School's Out, The Degrassi Movie. He said he hated it but we ended up having regular Degrassi nights, his idea. I bought him the t-shirt last Christmas and he wore it regularly.

He looked over to the laundry door and his face erupted with excitement to see me standing there.

"She's here," he seemed to say more to himself than anyone.

"Birthday Girl!" Luke cheered.

Thank you, world. I hadn't slept through it.

Evie squealed and Oakley said something like "my birthday girl," but I was too distracted by his new hair cut to catch it. The three of them rushed towards me and formed a circle around me, connecting us all in the same embrace. Oakley stood in front of me.

"You changed your hair style?" I half asked, half stated.

The corner of his mouth turned up. "I look pretty sexy, hey?"

"Only a little," I shyly teased.

The circle squeezed in tighter and began to bellow a truly awful rendition of Happy Birthday. Luke was a line behind every one else the whole way through, Evie tried too hard to sound like Lady Gaga and Oakley's hair distracted me from even noticing what he sounded like. It was the best recital of Happy Birthday I had ever heard.

Laughter erupted throughout my whole body and without even thinking I quoted a line from The Breakfast Club. Evie joyfully retorted the line right after.

"Point Evie!" I exclaimed.

"Wait, I need more," Luke panicked.

Oakley contributed his own quote from the scene in question. I was impressed.

"Breakfast Club!" Luke shouted.

"Duh," Evie rolled her eyes.

"I'm very aware that I'll never be able to keep up with your knowledge of all things eighties," Luke conceded.

We sat at the table and feasted until we nearly burst. Luke had made me his signature milkshake and stuck a Happy Birthday cake topper in the cream. It was a joyful start to the day. The four of us were together again. Ask any adult what they want for their birthday and the majority will just say that they want everyone to be together.

The time passed too quickly and suddenly eight thirty in the morning became ten thirty. Luke shared news of his firm's offer to make him a partner, Oakley was pissed that his landlord had put his house up for sale so he needed to find "new digs" and Evie was agonising over her current relationship status. She and Ryan had got together in Evie's second week in Sydney, so had been together almost six months. He worked in a petrol station and played the guitar in his band, The Devil Whisperers, who were apparently on the rise to fame in the Sydney hotel market.

"He acted so cold when we were at the airport," Evie whinged.

"Of course," Oakley replied, "he probably didn't want you to go."

"It's not like I'm moving to another country."

"Dude, he lives in a caravan in his parent's backyard!" Luke chimed in.

"That's just until he gets permanent gigs," Evie replied defensively.

"Just marry me instead," Luke smiled. "I don't even like caravans."

Evie laughed. "Don't you have a girlfriend now? Andrea?"

"Annabelle and yes, going on four months now, but she knows I'll always be in love with you first."

Oakley shifted in his seat. "So, you get two women who adore you and I go home every night to my goldfish."

"You could have a girlfriend," Luke replied, "but you block their calls as soon as you've slept with them."

A tense silence filled the air as we anxiously awaited Oakley's comeback. I searched his face for signs and he stared pensively across the backyard.

"I might mow the lawn for you." He stood from his spot on the ground, put his plate on the table and proceeded to make his way over to the shed where the lawnmower lived in solitude.

"He's serious," Evie chuckled. "He's actually going to mow our lawn!"

"Girlfriends are always a sore subject. I don't get it," Luke sighed. And then looked at me.

I shifted in my seat. "I might go have a shower if that's okay. I've got stuff at 12 before tea with Mum and Dad tonight. Thanks for the birthday breakfast, guys."

Evie and Luke continued to make fun of Oakley while he mowed the lawn. The window in the bathroom was open and so too the torn lace curtains. I stepped up onto the toilet seat to pull them shut. Out the window, a visibly annoyed Oakley pushed the lawn mower across our backyard. He ran over a pile of pegs and shards of plastic flew out from underneath.

"Fuck!" he shouted. "Fucking fuckitty fuck!"

Roars of laughter resonated from the patio and I giggled along. Oakley kicked the lawnmower and started pulling out the bits of plastic that were jammed in the rotor.

"Turn it off first, you dumb shit!" Luke yelled out.

The lawnmower grunted and Oakley exclaimed "fuck!" as leapt out of its way. Evie and Luke's laughter became uncontrollable. Oakley panted "shut up, I could have lost my hand!"

He was adorable when he was angry. I closed the curtains and smiled to myself.

I pulled out my stool from behind the towel rack and set it up in the shower. I was ready to wash away the depression that was yesterday and enjoy the last birthday the world would give me.

The water crashed onto my skin with too much force and I winced under its power. I sat on the stool and washed myself as quickly as my breath would allow.

When I got out of the shower, I heard Mum and Dad's voice in the kitchen with Evie's. I wrapped my towel around me and put my beanie back on before creeping down to my bedroom to get dressed. I was exhausted. I grabbed my mobile and SMSed Mum: Can you please help me get dressed? I'm aching and so tired.

Mum knocked on my door a millisecond after I had pressed send.

"Can I come in?"

"Of course, Mum," I answered breathlessly.

Mum came in and helped me get dressed. I felt like a raggedy Anne doll. My head felt heavy and it was an effort to hold it up. Mum pulled on my trackies and t-shirt and then walked behind me to the car, holding my waist. Dad and Evie waved us goodbye and Mum called out, "be back in a couple of hours!"

It was only a few minutes' drive to Melbourne Street. Mum helped me walk in, chit chatted to the regular office girls and I made myself comfy on the recliner. I pressed the remote to lift my legs up and positioned my arm on the rest, palm facing the ceiling. The nurse wheeled the intravenous pole next to me and started tapping my arm. I closed my eyes and slept while they pumped the usual fortnightly toxins straight into my bloodstream.

When I woke up, I was on my own bed, in my room. My legs were stretched across Mum's knees.

"Keep sleeping, my love," she softly spoke. "We've got a big evening. I'll wake you up in an hour."

Mum started humming and with the safety of knowing I wouldn't sleep the rest of my birthday away, I closed my eyes and let sleep come.

Soon a calm voice crept into my deep slumber. "Time to wake up, birthday girl."

I opened my eyes to the sight of Mum, still sitting across my bed.

"What time is it?"

"Just after four. I'll help you get dressed and then we'll do some presents!"

I smiled. Presents seemed ironic. Or maybe that's why they're called presents: they're just for right now, the present. Regardless of whether or not you actually have a future.

I walked over to my dressing table and rubbed moisturiser into my neck and arms. Mum brought over a red floral dress from my wardrobe.

"This one?"

I smiled as Mum excitedly held up the dress behind me.

"I used to love that dress, hey? Remember I wore it to Evie's uni graduation?" My smiled waned. "It might be a bit too baggy on me now. I was just going to wear my black trackies and a nice top."

"Let's see!"

Mum quickly slipped the dress over my head, ignoring everything I had just said. She spent much longer than necessary straightening out the shoulders and fiddling with the fit.

"Stunning!" she exclaimed theatrically.

I looked at my reflection in the mirror. I hadn't even contemplated wearing this dress in years. I remember the last time I wore it: it was my day off work but I had to go into the Nursing Home for training. I wore it over black tights with my black ballet flats. Oakley drove me to work that day because I had been feeling so exhausted the last few weeks and he insisted on driving me. When he picked me up, he instantly said, "you look beautiful, Mackenzie". I of course laughed him off and turned on the radio. It's strange, the details you remember. It was the first time a man had ever called me the b word. And he called me by my name, not just 'Mack.'

The training went for a good two hours but he waited for me. I had expected him to drive home and come back, or at least go to the shops to kill time, but he waited in the carpark for me. He sat in his car for two hours waiting for me.

He drove us to the beach after and we ate hot cinnamon doughnuts on the bonnet of his car. He made me laugh as he did his best John Bender impersonation with the magnificent waves crashing behind him. Hanging out with Oakley had become my favourite thing, being with him my happy place.

We ordered pizza when we got back to his house and played Scrabble until our eyes grew heavy.

"I should get going," I announced after whipping him by one hundred points. "I have a blood test tomorrow to find out why I'm so tired all the time."

"I can take you to that."

"Thanks, but Mum's good to go."

"You know, when I come back here after driving you home, I just know the scent of your perfume will still be here and it will make me miss you even more than I always do."

I bit my lip and smiled shyly. "I miss you too when I'm not with you."

I swallowed my nerves and reciprocated when he kissed me. I didn't want him to know that it was my first kiss. To know that I was twenty-four years old and this was my first kiss. Was his face meant to be this close to mine? I was so uncomfortable. I felt ridiculously self-conscious. Was I doing it right? I wasn't sure if this is what it was meant to feel like. He pulled his lips away slowly and locked eyes with me.

"I have wanted to kiss you since the day I came looking for you after Solli's."

Oh my.

He cupped my cheeks in his hands and kissed me again, and I think I gasped. I closed my eyes and followed his lead. It felt more natural this time and I mentally congratulated myself for getting it right on only my second try. His kiss was consuming. I don't know why people say you get butterflies in your tummy, because they were wreaking havoc in my knees. If he wasn't holding onto me, I would have surely toppled over.

I looked over to the track suit pants scrunched up on my bed.

"This is you," Mum whispered, still fiddling with the dress as I stood in front of the mirror. "You look like you again."

I was going to wear the dress simply for her, and she knew it. My mind screamed for my trackies but I knew Mum needed me to wear something else today.

"I have a little present, just from me."

Mum picked up a small parcel from the bed, wrapped in paper plastered with love hearts. "It's just from me."

I ran my palm over the gift as it rested in Mum's hands. Mum watched me eagerly. I didn't know what it was, but I did know that it was important to her for some reason. I unwrapped it gleefully.

"Mum," I exclaimed, running my hand across the corduroy material, "this is so cool. Thank you, I love it."

"Will you wear it tonight?" Mum asked hopefully, tugging gently at my faithful white beanie.

"Of course," I almost stuttered.

The thought of wearing anything other than my white beanie absolutely terrified me. But the thought of making this horrible cancer shit harder on Mum than it already was terrified me more. I broke her heart every day and I owed it to her. Especially on my birthday. On my last birthday.

"No trackies today. No white beanie today," Mum whispered as she snuggled into my neck. She kissed my cheek and her whole face beamed. "My birthday girl. I'll meet you in the lounge."

She left my room and I whispered "won't be long" to the door as she quietly closed it.

I studied myself in the mirror. Cue music: Little Birdy, Beautiful To Me. I took off my white beanie and slipped my trendy new black corduroy cap onto my smooth head. I decided on my black ankle boots. May as well do the full look. Ugg boots probably wouldn't match the vibe Mum was aiming for.

I stared at my red floral dress as it fell off my skinny frame. Looking into the mirror was like bumping into someone you used to know but can't quite figure out how. If I didn't have cancer, I would have almost looked like me again. The thing is, I didn't want to look like me. I didn't want to look like me until I was me.

"For you, Mum," I said out loud to my reflection. I smiled longingly at my trackies on the bed, blew them a kiss, and headed out to the lounge.

I was more nervous than what would be considered healthy. I had worn my white beanie and trackies for so long that they were a part of me. They were my cancer outfit. I didn't know who I was anymore outside of being the one with cancer. The daughter with cancer. The sister with cancer. The friend with cancer. The roommate with cancer. It was just who I was now.

Mum and Dad sat together on the couch. Oakley was sitting on the carpeted floor in front of them and Luke sat on the arm of Evie's chair. Everyone was chatting happily and stopped in silence when I entered the room.

I looked to Oakley first. He frowned ever so slightly and then his mouth opened as if he was forcing out a breath. It was nice the way he looked at me. I liked it too much. Feeling brave, I smiled and held out the hem of my dress in a curtsey. Pretty sure I just flirted with him. I was so damn proud I had to mentally restrain myself from fist pumping the air.

I had wondered if he would remember the dress but the way he raised his eyebrows and tilted his head told me that indeed he did.

"Hubba Bubba Miss 30," Luke teased.

Evie smiled. "There you are again. Birthdays look good on you! You should have them more often." She instantly choked on her words. "Shit. That didn't sound like I meant it to. Shit. Sorry."

I looked to Mum who had her head bowed low.

"Sorry Mum," Evie quickly added. "I didn't mean it like that."

I laughed to break the deadening silence that filled the room.

"It's not funny," Mum smiled.

She smiled, so I don't really give a shit whether it was funny or not.

"Let's do presents!" Oakley blurted out. Thankfully.

I sat next to him on the floor, why I'm not really sure. I always want to be close to him but never know how to go about it. Apparently, my dress does though.

"I'll go first!" Evie placed a parcel wrapped in pink unicorn paper in my lap. I gleefully ripped into it to reveal a basket of vanilla candles. My favourite scent and my favourite luxury.

"I love this, thank you."

Mum and Dad gave me lots of new books, chocolates, a bag, DVDs and a delicate gold necklace with a dandelion on it.

"Never stop wishing," Dad said as he kissed my cheek.

"Thank you, everything is perfect."

"My turn!" Luke placed a huge parcel across my lap. "Size matters, hey Oaks."

"What are you, 16?" Evie laughed and smacked Luke on his leg.

He rested his head on her shoulder. "That would make you my cougar."

Mum and Dad chuckled.

I ripped Luke's present open and gasped as I saw it. It was a painting of a Cherry Blossom tree.

"I love this so much," I declared, wiping away a tear.

"I can top it!" Oakley reached behind me and pulled out his present. It was wrapped in yellow paper, my favourite colour. I carefully peeled off the sticky tape and folded the wrapping paper back. I didn't want to ruin anything Oakley gave me.

"Oh my god!" I squealed. "Oh my god! This is insane! How did you do this?"

I held up Oakley's present for everyone to see. It was a t-shirt with Molly Ringwald on it, as she is in Pretty in Pink. Only my face had been photoshopped onto Molly's body.

Mum and Dad clapped their hands.

"That's pretty impressive," Luke admitted with a laugh.

"I seriously can't tell you how much I love this!" I excitedly announced.

"Would you just hurry up and marry him?" Evie joked.

I choked on my own spit. "Is anyone as hungry as I am? Is it din dins time?"

"Wait, I have one more!" Evie ran to her room to retrieve a gold envelope. Placing it on my lap, she knelt in front of me and cupped my knees with her hands.

"Do you remember when you were fourteen and you got sick for the first time? Remember that night laying on the trampoline, the night you got home from your first chemo treatment, and you told me that you wanted to die soon so that Mum, Dad and me wouldn't have to suffer too long? Because

I do. I have thought about that night every single night of my life since."

Tears burned my flushed cheeks.

"And do you remember what I told you?" she continued. "When you said it would be better for us if you died, I told you to fuck off with that thinking. We both freaked out a little because that was the first time either one of us had said fuck. We were scared shitless that Mum might have heard, remember that? And then the whole motivational speaker vibe kicked in and I went on and on about how fucking amazing this thing called life is. Life is fucking amazing, Mack. It was then and it is now. Don't live to die. Fucking die to live!"

My eyes widened as I thought back to that night and I realised where Evie was heading with this. "Oh shit!"

Evie threw her head back in a theatrical laugh.

"You remember it too, don't you? Our promise!"

I shook my head in disbelief. "Evie! We are not!"

"Yep. Yep, we are!"

I literally screamed. And then Evie screamed. And then Mum screamed and she didn't even know why.

Oakley sat up on his knees. "What? What did you promise?"

I grabbed Evie's hands and shook them vigorously. "We're going to jump out of a fucking plane!" I screamed.

A collective gasp filled the room. "Oh my god," Mum whispered to herself.

Evie held onto my hands tightly. "I told my baby sister that night that she was going to live. She didn't believe me. She said she was so scared to die, more scared than anything else I could imagine. I joked and said 'what about jumping out of a plane?' and she agreed that that would probably be worse. I promised her with everything I had that she was going to survive. And that we would jump out of a plane on her 30th birthday, to prove that she was going to make it that far and that she is a goddamn hero who can conquer the scariest shit life throws at you."

I shook my head in disbelief. "Evie, I'm going to pass out on the way down!"

"This is going to be so brilliant!" Luke laughed, "Oaks and I will be on the ground getting drunk!"

"I told you you would get here," Evie whispered to me.

I threw my torso into her and wrapped my arms around her. "We're going to make such a spectacle of ourselves up there!"

"So be it! Let's friggin live! Experience everything life has to offer because it is only as amazing as we allow it to be."

"I'll drink to that! Cheers everybody! Happy Birthday, Mackenzie!" Dad raised his glass and everyone applauded.

I sank back in my chair, mentally exhausted and in total shock.

The buzz continued as everyone chatted excitedly and swapped stories of their week so far. Mum soon stood up and motioned for everyone to do the same. "Come on, reservation is at six."

Evie and Mum locked up the house and then drove off with Dad in his car. I rode shotgun with Luke. Oakley carried on how about "how disappointed" he was that his favourite girl didn't get a rose in last night's The Bachelor episode.

"She was only in it for the insta followers," I enlightened him.

We pulled up to the red light, stationed next to a red Kia cramped with perky teenagers, no doubt heading into town for the night. They persistently motioned for Oakley to roll his window down, presumably so they could chat him up. Luke teased him relentlessly, encouraging him to "give the jail bait something to tweet about," and I probably didn't help by laughing so much. Oakley really didn't like attention. He seemed annoyed with the world, but managed to smile sweetly at them when the light changed to green.

"Thank fuck for that," he muttered under his breath. Moody bugger.

Dinner was at my favourite restaurant down at Glenelg. It was Saturday night and hence there were far too many people here for my level of comfort. I felt massively self-conscious without my white beanie and my paranoia was skyrocketing. I tugged at my black beret as we took our seats and we all browsed the menu. We had ordered within a few minutes and the conversation flew smoothly while we waited.

Talk inevitably switched to my appointment and Mum filled everyone in on Doctor Young's recommendation that we try stem cell treatment therapy as I had built up an immunity to the chemo and radiation. Evie said she had been googling it and it sounded very promising if I was deemed a good candidate. I was grateful when our meals were finally served.

I ordered the pasta alio olio and it was divine. I could have easily eaten another bowl. I tugged at my beanie for the hundredth time that hour as I scooped up the remnants of the sauce.

"Stop fiddling with it," Mum quietly instructed, "it looks good."

"I just feel awkward, I'm not used to it."

"That's because..." Evie gave a dramatic pause as if she was building up to something and then proceeded to literally sing; "you're insecure."

"Don't know what for," Oakley instantly sang in reply.

My whole face smiled.

"You're turning heads when you walk through the doo-o-or," Luke joined in.

"Oh my god!" I blushed in embarrassment.

Just when I thought my little serenade was done, Dad abruptly leapt to his feet and burst into tune. "Everyone else in the room could see it! Everyone else but you-oo-oo!"

And then my whole family stood around the table, grooving their way through their One Direction tribute to me. Evie, Luke, Oakley, Mum and Dad sang at the top of their lungs, right in the middle of the restaurant. I looked up at them in awe as they belted and boogied their way through their animated performance. I was utterly speechless and very aware that I was in the throes of having the best moment of my life.

The whole restaurant started to clap along and even the waiting staff were dancing between the tables. I felt goose bumps shiver up my arms and I pressed my lips together to supress my squeals of excitement. I was in disbelief that such an insanely amazing scene could even happen outside of the movies, in real life. In my real life.

"The way that you mmmm at the mmm it mmmmm mmmm to tell," Mum improvised.

They sang together, so loud I wondered if they actually had hidden microphones in their clothing.

"YOU DON'T KNOW OHOHOH! YOU DON'T KNOW YOU'RE BEAUTIFUL! OH! THAT'S WHAT MAKES YOU BEAUTIFUL!"

The entire restaurant erupted into applause. People were actually whistling and stomping their feet. For once I didn't even mind that everyone was staring at me. Evie's laughter reigned supreme. She was so proud of herself; obviously the mastermind behind the whole thing. I imagined her trying to teach Mum and Dad the lyrics over the past few days and I couldn't help but laugh right alongside her.

Dad put his arms over Oakley and Luke's shoulders; the three of them just radiated happiness. Mum ran over to my side of the table, fidgeted with my beret as if making fun of me and gave me a smile full of so much love I could feel it in my soul. Evie is so right; how fucking amazing is this thing called life?

We stood up to leave while the whole restaurant cheered on. Oakley bowed and Evie and Luke grooved all the way to the door. We were still on a high when we reached the cars.

"I didn't get to finish my bottle of champagne!" Dad teased.

Evie and Luke seated themselves in the back of Mum and Dad's car to my surprise, so I got into Luke's car with Oakley.

"Drive carefully, please," Mum sternly instructed as she popped her head through my passenger window.

"Don't worry Ma, I've only had one bottle of Jack and a joint to wash it down with," Oakley coolly replied.

Dad chuckled and Mum ignored him.

"Happy Birthday, baby girl," Mum and Dad both said as they crouched alongside the open window of the car. "We love you to bits."

"Love you more," I confidently replied.

Oakley slowly drove off and beeped twice. I looked in the side mirror to see Mum and Dad joyfully dancing in the street.

"Are you too tired to make a little detour?" Oakley asked.

"I'm intrigued."

Five minutes later, we were parked in the street looking out onto the beach. It was only eight o'clock but the warmth from the day lingered on. For such a warm evening, the beach was surprisingly empty. It was just us and it felt like it.

Oakley turned off the engine and reached across to unclick my seat belt. "Want to watch the waves with me?"

We got out of the car and I stared out at the beach, breathing in the dominant aura of the waves as they seduced the sand. Oakley magically produced a blanket and laid it over the bonnet of Luke's car. He scooped me up in his arms and gently sat me on the blanket. Standing in front of me, he smiled to himself. "I planned this."

I bit my lip. "Yeah, I get that impression."

Cue music: Cindy Lauper, I Drove All Night. Oakley's breath hastened. "I forgot to get doughnuts."

I giggled and he smiled at the sound. His eyes fixated on my lips. My breathing accelerated to match his. Oakley moved his face closer to mine and rested his forehead against me. His breath was warm. I realised that he was going to kiss me and my eyes widened in fear. I think he sensed my panic and worried that my flight mode would kick in because he suddenly kissed me with such haste and abandonment that it made me gasp in his mouth. His lips were laden with a desperate passion and I melted into his face. He kissed me harder and pulled my torso flush up against his own. My whole body came alive and I was hungry for more of this feeling. He rushed a hand to the back of my head and held me to him. He clutched at my hips and frantically kissed me as if an alarm would sound any second. I had to discipline myself from squealing with delight.

For years I have been living in preparation to die. Even with all the cancer in my body, I can't imagine feeling more alive than right now.

I gasped as his hand slid my dress up my thighs. He touched me and I inhaled so deeply I think I swallowed the entire atmosphere around me. He grasped my underwear with both hands and passionately pulled them out from under me, slipping them down my legs and tucking them in his shirt pocket. I laughed as he lunged at my lips again. He kissed so hard, so desperately. I couldn't keep up. I moved my head to the side and he traced his mouth up and down my neck. I tried to catch my breath while I could.

I felt his sides, his shape. I pushed him back a little and put my hands under his shirt. His abdomen was hard, contoured. I glided my hands over him as he undid his buttons. He smiled as I blushed at his body.

I giggled and he kissed me again, slower. He put his hands on my hips and pulled me into him.

I inhaled deeply. "Oakley."

He started moving in and out and I grasped onto him. My legs were tingling. I was completely his.

"Is this okay?" he panted.

"Yes," I could only whisper back.

He nuzzled into my neck as he kept moving my body with his. His lips moved to my mouth but I quickly turned my head away and exhaled slowly, trying to blow away the vomit that was rising up my throat.

"Stop!" I hastily exclaimed.

Oakley instantly stopped moving and looked at me in shock.

"Really?" he laughed.

I looked away in embarrassment and rested my forehead on his shoulder. "It's making me feel sick."

Oakley nudged his shoulder up, lifting my face to meet his. "I'm making you feel sick?"

My legs held their pose, hugging his thighs. I was so embarrassed and bit my lip nervously.

"The moving back and forth," I said shyly, "it's making me feel nauseous. I'd rather not throw up on you. We need to stop."

Oakley smirked. "I don't think I can stop."

He kissed me long and hard and started moving our bodies together again, slowly. I breathed deeply and allowed myself to love it. But merely moments later the ball of vomit reappeared in my throat. It wanted out. I quickly put my hand across Oakley's mouth and whispered, "I can't." He stopped moving and embraced me. I rested my head on his shoulder and cried.

"I'm so sorry. This is so embarrassing," I sobbed.

He didn't say anything for what felt like eternity. He just hugged me and I just cried.

"I don't know how to pull myself away from you," he finally whispered. "The second I do; you will be gone. Like always. Can I just stay here for a bit longer?"

Cue music: Paloma Faith, Only Love Can Hurt Like This.

I snuggled into his neck and we stayed in our embrace. Connected.

"I'll drive you home," he finally mumbled.

Oakley stepped back from me and zipped up his jeans. Without looking at me, he took my hand and helped me step off the boot. We got back in the car and drove in silence. It was excruciating. He didn't take his eyes off the road and held the steering wheel so tightly I was sure the rubber would peel off under his grasp. When we got to my house, he said softly, "wait there" and then came around and opened my door. He reached his hand out and I rose from my seat with my hand in his. He didn't lift his eyes from the ground as he kissed my cheek and said "good night, birthday girl." He got back in the car and drove off without another word or glance.

I stood in the street and listened to the end of the song in my head.

"Shit! My friggin undies!"

The fourth chapter

I woke up the next day to the sound of Evie crying in her room. I reached for my sick pot and violently vomited up the nausea that was invading my stomach. I slipped on my trackies and beanie, carefully carried the pot down to the bathroom, tipped the bile down the toilet, brushed my teeth, gargled and followed the sound of howls down to Evie's room.

I knocked and entered without waiting for her reply. Evie was sitting on the floor in front of her bed.

"Finally! I've been crying for an hour!"

Photos were tossed all over the floor. I picked one up; a selfie of Evie and what's-his-name stared intensely at me. I joined Evie on the floor and we rested our heads together. I sat in silence while she cried.

"He broke up with you," I half asked, half stated.

Through soggy breaths, Evie told me how "that asshole" had broken up with her over the phone last night. They had skyped after my birthday dinner, during which Evie heard a woman's voice call out from his kitchen, "Hey Ry, where do you keep the glasses?"

"He tried to tell me it was his mother for fuck's sake!" Evie blew her nose on a tissue and slammed it into the floor. "I'm such an idiot. I got all excited and said 'wow, can I meet her?'"

I couldn't help but giggle. "What did he say to that?"

Evie put on a macho voice, "Oh yeah…um…Mum would love that! Hey Mum, shout out 'hello' to Evie! Fucker."

"Did she say hello?" I chuckled.

"Don't laugh!" Evie pressed her lips together to supress her own chuckle. "Yes. Yes, she did. She called out 'oh hi, Mum!' Dipshit. So, he fucking panicked and said 'such a joker, aren't you, Mum? You mean hi, Evie. You're Mum!' Oh my god. Like how stupid does he think I am?"

"More like how stupid are they?"

"And fucking Devil Whisperers? What kind of fucked up name is that? Like they're admitting they have one-on-one chats with the fucking devil? Hope that tart doesn't wear a crucifix!" Evie blew her nose and slammed down another fistful of tissues.

My favourite thing about my sister is her passion. She is full of love or full of hate. No in-between.

I draped my arm across her shoulders and rested my head against her neck.

"I love you," I said softly.

"I love you, too, little sis." She took a long, deep breath. "Maybe I should just give in and marry Luke?"

"Your children would be ridiculously good looking."

"Yeah," she said with a touch of sadness in her voice. "If only I loved him that way."

We sat on Evie's bedroom floor continuing to man-bash and toy with life's what ifs.

"Where did Oakley take you last night? He asked me if I could drive home with everyone else so he obviously wanted to be alone with you."

"We went to the beach, well the car park at the beach. Our usual spot."

"Your usual spot, hey?" Evie beamed.

"We get hot cinnamon doughnuts and eat them in the car, or on the car, and just listen to the waves. I love the beach, he hates the beach. It's a nice compromise."

"A nice compromise would be for you to just let him fuck you already."

"Oh my god ssh! Don't talk like that. You know we're just friends."

"And you know that he wants more than that."

"And you know that I can't give him more than that."

"And you know that I don't agree with that."

"And you know that you would do the same if you were me."

"And you know, damn well, that I would do the total opposite if I were you."

I took her hand in mine and rested it on my leg. "If you were dying, would you really take the one you love along for the ride?"

"Fuck!" Evie jumped out of her skin. "You just said you love him!"

My eyes widened. "No! I didn't! I didn't mean it like that. Shit. You know what I mean."

"Yeah, I know what you mean, Mack." Evie held my eyes with her own. "He can handle it. He is going to suffer regardless of whether you let him know how you feel."

I am very aware that I am dying, and soon. But whatever you believe about what happens after death, that's where the pain of dying ends for me. Mum, Dad, Evie, Luke, Oakley; they're the ones who will have to live with the pain for the rest of their lives. Surely it will hurt less to lose a friend than to lose a lover? To lose someone you care about as opposed to someone you love. To lose someone you hang out with over someone you are intimately connected to.

"It's just better this way, dude," I assured her and myself.

Suddenly, Evie's door burst open. Oakley and Luke jumped into the middle of the room, wearing nothing but their socks and jocks. Evie and I shot a bemused look at each other and had a quick perve on the pretty impressive torsos presented before us.

They stood on the other side of the room with their hands on their hips, in their half naked glory, seeming to be waiting for some sort of a cue.

I was speechless. Evie took the initiative; "Um, what the actual fuck?"

Oakley brought his finger to his lips and motioned for silence, which evidently pissed Evie off.

"Don't ssh me!" she snapped.

Luke rolled his eyes as he propped his phone on Evie's bed and pressed the screen, making The Eurythmics' Thorn in My Side resonate around the room at full volume. Luke and Oakley began to mime into their fisted hands and step in time to the beat.

Evie and I roared with laughter. The boys mimed along to Annie Lennox and moved their perfectly sculptured torsos in rhythm. They even had a hastily choreographed dance routine going on. Their performance was like an audition for Priscilla, Queen of the Desert.

Evie squealed and laughed and clapped and cheered as both of the boys kept their eyes fixated on her and fed off her energy. It was brilliant.

The end of the song came too soon and the boys took their bow. Oakley left without saying a word or gesturing a wave. Luke paused in the doorway.

"He is a dickhead. Not worth your tears or another second of your time. Now if you'll excuse me, I have to meet up with a very important client."

"Perhaps clothes?" Evie giggled.

Luke winked in reply and left to get ready for his meeting.

"Hey, those cheap bastards didn't give us an encore!" Evie hummed what appeared to be her new-found favourite song and set about tidying up the collection of tissues and ripped up selfies from the floor. The vibe that lingered in the room almost made her look happy while she did it.

I gazed at the door and muttered "nice" to myself in realisation that Oakley hadn't looked in my direction once the entire time he was here. I knew that for certain because I hadn't taken my eyes off of him.

I left Evie to merrily clean up her mess and headed out the room to look for Oakley. He wasn't on the couch like I expected him to be. I heard a clang of keys and turned to the front door just in time to see Oakley closing it behind him.

I could have left it there. I guess. But I was slightly pissed off. I checked my beanie felt properly in place and charged out the door after him.

"Oakley!"

Oakley was standing by his car, zipping up his jeans. "What's wrong? Are you okay? Do you feel sick?"

I was trying to be mad at him and him being all concerned and thoughtful wasn't helping.

"I'm f-f-fine." My frown relaxed as Oakley stepped towards me. "I just, I just…"

I couldn't even articulate a sentence. I love you. I have been in love with you for nine years. I can't be with you because I don't want you to suffer more than you are already going to when I die. Because I am going to die. Soon. I want to be with you forever but my forever is so short compared to yours. I am so in love with you. Please know that. I push you away because I am scared shitless of dying and loving you makes the thought of dying so much worse.

"You still have my undies."

Oakley smirked. "What makes you think I intend to give them back?"

I slapped him on his bicep and held onto it longer than was perhaps required in that particular moment.

"Why didn't you talk to me when we got back last night? And you didn't even look at me this morning! It's like I wasn't even there! You can't have sex with a girl and then treat her like that! Like dude, that's really shitty! You have no right to be mad at me!" The words spilled out of my mouth before my brain could assess the need for censorship. "I'm sorry I can't be who you want me to be! It's not my fault!"

I was out of breath and wasn't aware that I was crying until I instinctively wiped the tears that stung my flushed cheeks.

"You think this is about sex?" Oakley shook his head in annoyance. "You can't be who I want you to be? Are you fucking serious? I have tried! I accept you for who you are and all the fucked up shit that comes with it! I have never said I can't do it, can't deal with it! Never told you I can't be with you because you're sick. I wanted to be with you before all that shit and I still want to be with you during it. You won't let me! You! You are the one who convinces yourself that you can't be who I want you to be! I. Want. You. I have never run away from this, from us! I have never told you we can't be together because you're sick! I. Have. Tried! And every single time we get close to making this work, you! You are the one who pulls the plug! Every fucking time! You let me think we can finally be together and then BAM! You run!"

I swallowed and the sound was deafening against the silence that filled the air.

"It's you, Mack. You are the one who says we can't be together. And every time, I get through it. In complete secret. Every time I act as if it's okay. Every time I carry on as if nothing has changed and I'm completely fine when all I want to do is lay down and cry. Because if I don't, then I'm the asshole, right? Because of the cancer, I'm the asshole. Well you know what? You're the asshole here, Mack. Not me. You know damn well that you would have given me your usual 'I can't be with you like this' speech after last night."

My mouth dropped open ready to speak but the words hid in the pit of my stomach. He reached for my hand and clasped it between both of his.

"You can pretend nothing changes every time we almost get there. But I can't keep doing this and you know why, Mack. I am in love with you and you fucking know it."

My heart ached and I frantically searched his face for signs of a smile. I needed him to quote Pretty in Pink or give me his best Drop Dead Fred impersonation. He dropped his head and released my hand from his grip.

"Just give me a day or two hey? I'll come see you next week at the hospital and we'll be okay. Remember? We do 'okay' pretty good."

He walked back to his car and opened the door roughly. He revved his engine and drove off without his usual double honk goodbye, for the second time in two days.

I stared at the empty road after him and slowed my breaths. My friggin undies. I turned back to the house and lifted my head from the ground.

"What the fuck, Mack?" Evie stood by the open front door with her arms folded. "Evidently there are some things you need to tell me."

The fifth chapter

"Your veins are playing hide and seek this morning."

The nurse continued to tap my wrist while Mum rubbed my feet anxiously. I stared up at the ceiling and concentrated on the music playing in my head. I had gone through the entire list of songs from New Kids on the Block's Greatest Hits before she coolly announced, "that should be enough." She picked up the three tubes of my blood, pulled the blanket up to my chin and instructed me to lay still for twenty minutes.

I wondered what her name was. It seemed like such a one-sided relationship; she knew intimate details about me, to the point of knowing how many cells are in my blood, and I don't even know her name. Was that my bad for not asking her or her bad for not telling me?

Nurse No Name left my room and Mum came to stand by my side. Poetic really when I think about it.

"You did good, baby. I feel good about this."

"What do we have to do next?"

We were exploring "the other option," as Doctor Young had put it. Something to do with reprogramming my cells. I personally didn't feel words like "exciting" and "opportunity" were appropriate descriptions but the team of doctors who kept analysing my charts seemed to think they were. Doctor Young said that "at the very least, every patient helps us fine tune the process." I resented those words and the obligation they eluded to.

"Doctor Young will be in soon and she'll go through it all with us."

Mum's eyes looked hopeful. If she was a cartoon, they would have been drawn with a shiny white star on them. Personally, I had no interest at all in being a pioneer for something, in spending my last days on earth cooped up in a hospital room so the doctors could play with me and potentially save someone else one day. The twinkle was my motivation. I couldn't care less about helping anyone else at this point. Particularly because they would get to live and I don't. I was only here to keep that twinkle in Mum's eyes.

My hospital room was perhaps the nicest one I had stayed in since this became who I was all those years ago. I took in the space around me; the luxury bathroom, the kitchenette, the lounge...it had an undeniable hospice feel to it. People, many, probably lost their life right here in this room and here I was, ironically, clutching at anything that could save mine. I came here to live but this is where you come to die.

Mum got herself cosy on the couch and switched on the unnecessarily large TV affixed to the wall. Dr Phil started shouting about priorities and Mum wiggled herself into the cushion.

"I say, this is comfy!"

I chuckled and closed my eyes and dozed off to the sound of Dr Phil's buzz words floating across the room.

"You have to understand that the chances of the treatment taking to Mackenzie's body are incredibly slim. Her cancer is widespread and has developed an immunity to treatment. She is in the final stages. This is an exciting opportunity to test this therapy and ascertain it's strength amidst terminal diagnosis."

The two words I have come to loathe, 'exciting' and 'opportunity', teamed with the insulting insinuation that I was merely 'research.' I opened my eyes to see Mum and Doctor Young standing on either side of the bed. Mum helped me sit up and propped my pillows behind me.

"Prepare to be here for a couple of weeks. We need to obtain sufficient samples and get an increased regime of chemo up and running before the re-engineered cells are ready in a few weeks. We hope to have them sent off by Friday. It is imperative that you keep up your fluids. You have chemo tomorrow and next Monday we'll do the surgery to replace your PICC so we can increase your chemo in the lead up to the cell transplant. The couch opens up as a bed, so you are welcome to have one visitor stay with you overnight. Communication is essential, as I always tell you. Please tell me how you are feeling, both physically and emotionally. You need to stay on top of your mental health, too. There have been a lot of studies linking a positive mindset to the effectiveness of treatment."

Doctor Young handed me a pink journal with gold flecks etched onto the cover.

"Please write in this as much as you can. Your emotions, how you feel physically. It could really help you, Mackenzie. You don't talk much to me in terms of how you are coping, so please try this."

I rested the gold flecked journal on my knees and stared at the muted image on the television. The Bold and the Beautiful. Ridge was looking pensively at Brooke, just as he was ten years ago when I last watched it, as if they have been living on pause all these years. I could relate.

Doctor Young sat herself next to me on the bed, reading my expression as I fixated on Brooke's ageless face. She patted the blanket that covered my legs.

"Tea will be delivered soon. I will be in to see you in the morning."

I nodded and watched Ridge storm out the door, the same time as Doctor Young saw herself out.

Brooke started to cry and if my Mum wasn't in the room, I would have cried along with her.

"Hey, hey, hey, beauties!" I looked to the door to see Evie bouncing through. Mum rushed up to greet her and they hugged with joy.

"How was it back at your old office today? Come sit, give me your bag."

"Wonderful, like I never left. I had to scare some perky little intern off my seat but other than that, nothing had changed. I still rule the office."

Mum stroked Evie's hair. "I'm going to get a coffee from downstairs now you're here. Do you want anything?"

"I'm good, I had a sub on the way."

Mum kissed me on the forehead. "I'll be back soon."

Mum grabbed her handbag and left the room in search of coffee. I stood up from the bed and stretched my body to the ceiling. Evie flopped on the couch.

"Have you spoken to him yet?" she asked playfully.

I rolled my track suit pants up to my knees and sat down next to her. I draped my legs across her lap and she did a drum roll on my shins.

"I rang him this morning and he didn't answer so I just left a message. I think I may have actually pushed him away for good this time."

"I still can't believe this has been going on for all these friggin years! And you never bloody told me!" Evie leant over and poked me in the tummy. "Honestly, Mack, as far as I was aware, you were a virgin."

I laughed self-consciously. "Don't say that word, you know I hate it. And you know I don't like talking about that stuff so ssh!"

"Maybe if you had tried talking to me years ago you wouldn't have got into this mess!"

"You're probably right there," I resigned.

"Is it just him? Or is my supposedly shy sister really an undercover slut?"

I laughed and slapped her hand.

"Far out! Yes, it's just him! Only him. He was my first kiss, but he doesn't know that, thank God. And of course, my first time, which he no doubt gathered. I can't say first boyfriend because I don't know if that's what he was, what we were. Just my first everything. And last, because I'm dying so none of this matters anyway."

I tried to sound nonchalant but inside my heart broke a little more.

"If you weren't dying, would he still be your last?"

Yes. I knew that for certain. I could never even think about being with anyone but him. "Who knows."

Our first kiss was literally days before I got the diagnosis and I basically broke up with him as soon as they told me I was sick. He protested, of course. Told me he wanted to be with me and we would get through it together but I wanted to do it on my own. I never really thought about how it must have felt for him, to hurt in secret, to have to hide his pain. To be around his friends and not let them know that he needed support. I never really thought about a lot of things. I went into robotic mode. I had cancer; any energy, time, thought, emotion...all of it had to be on reserve to fight. If I spent some of my energy on someone else, would that mean I had less ammunition to fight with?

Four weeks later, after my first round of chemotherapy, I kissed him right in the middle of Sixteen Candles. He kissed me back, really hard. I made him promise to keep us a secret. Looking back, I don't even know why really. Maybe I thought everyone would think I was selfish for making him be with me. And all my public energy was put into making sure I didn't smell like vomit. It was exhausting trying to keep everything together.

Less than three months after Sixteen Candles, I broke up with him. Again. And then it became a perpetual circle. I would tell him I needed to be on my own to concentrate on getting better. We would break up for a few months. Then the reality of my destiny would hit me, I didn't want to die alone, I wanted to feel something good, I missed him, I wanted to pretend the cancer didn't exist, I craved his touch, I was addicted to the way he made me feel, it was my birthday...there was always some reason that led me back to him. In my mind I was the ugliest, most repulsive, undesirable woman on the planet. No hair, no curves, barely any life left inside of me. And Oakley wanted me. He desired me. He pursued me. Holy shit did that feel amazing.

Mum came back with a coffee and two hot chocolates. She sat on my bed and the three of us chatted about everything except Oakley and cancer.

"Knock, knock!" A young uni-student-looking guy carried a tray over to the table. "Evening meal, ma'am. Enjoy."

Evie excitedly jumped up and bolted for the table.

"Oooh, what did you get?" She lifted the lid of the warmer to reveal a delicious looking vegetarian lasagne. "Jealous. Eat it before I do."

I was famished. I was always hungry. Mum and Evie joined me at the table.

"We can go thirds?" I offered.

"No dear, you eat it," Mum insisted. "I've got a chicken roll in the fridge and Evie had a sub, plus I've left her a doughnut at home."

"Ooh, thanks Mummy!" Evie clapped. "Are you sure you don't want me to stay here tonight, Mum? You've been here all day." Evie exchanged looks with Mum.

"I'm fine, Evie. I want to be here. You're on sleepover duty tomorrow night."

I ate my tea while Evie filled in Mum on her new-found hatred for Ryan and The Devil Whisperers. She used the f word more than she usually did in front of Mum, who tensed her lips with every uttering.

After I had devoured my last mouthful, Mum urged Evie to get going before it got dark. Evie hugged us both and Mum walked her down to the carpark. I used the time alone to brush my teeth, wash my face and put on my PJs. I smiled to myself as I fastened the buttons, recalling them being slowly undone by someone else once upon a lifetime ago.

Mum came back and did the same; brushed her teeth and put her PJs on. She settled me into bed, fussing over the blankets and pillows, before pulling the bed out of the couch for herself. She snuggled in and aimed the remote at the T.V.

"Okay, let's see."

Mum flicked through the same five channels twice before announcing the contenders.

"We've got Twilight on nine, Mission Impossible on seven and, ah forget it! We're watching this!"

Susan Sarandon exclaimed "Oh my!" and Mum squealed in delight. "Tally ho!"

I laughed and quizzed Mum about whether she preferred Bull Durham or White Palace.

"Bull Durham, but only because of Kevin."

I don't remember when I fell asleep but I woke up the next morning to the echo of Mum's peaceful snore.

"Love you," I whispered. "I'm sorry."

The sixth chapter

So, I guess I'll start as everyone does with these things.

Dear Diary,

I like your gold flecks. Probably the only reason I decided to write in you after all is because of your gold flecks. That, and Dr Young is intimidating in that regard: you want to do as she asks. She is immaculate in every way. It feels validating if she is not disappointed in you. Even more so if she actually likes you.

It's day three today. Wednesday. I am very tired. A bit stir crazy. A bit sick of my own company. Mum went home after breakfast yesterday. Evie stayed the night and went to work early this morning. Mum is coming back after lunch for the night shift. I wonder if it feels like that for them; a shift I mean. Like work.

I started on some new pills yesterday. Not sure how they are any different to my usual cocktail of skittles but they are a bit smaller so that's a bonus. Wishing I had one of Luke's milkshakes to wash them down with.

I've been googling about the cell treatment. I'm sure if I asked, Dr Young would love to explain it to me but I don't want to hear the words from an actual person. I would rather just read it on my own, from something incapable of spawning feelings of pity.

I haven't heard from Oakley. This is the first time that he has ever stopped talking to me. I am terrified that I have pushed him away for good. I guess I took it for granted that he would always come back.

I just don't want him to suffer more than he is already going to when I go. Why should I let him love me, only to lose me? And selfishly, leaving this life before I am ready is painful enough as it is. I don't need someone else to make it feel even more painful. Someone else to add weight to the mass of devastation I already carry around every day.

I have tried to hide the truly ugly side of all this from him; the vomiting, the itching, the depression, the fatigue, the odours, the aches...the dying. And it is exhausting. The small doses he does get a glimpse of are already too much.

My stomach feels strange. Like I have ants eating my stomach lining. I feel sore. My arms ache. My feet feel heavy.

I want to go in my sleep. I don't want to be aware when I die. To actually realise that I am taking my last breath. Far out, how terrifying. I can't imagine and yet I can. Please, just let me go in my sleep.

You know when you are really distraught, really traumatised or stressed, or sad or angry; well, I've always believed that if you can get through a whole song, keeping the beat, dancing your heart out, singing along, it means you will get through it. That's what I reckon anyway, always practised. When I got my diagnosis for the second time around, I blared You Win Again by The Bee Gees. I danced for the whole song; crying, slobbering, screaming, but I danced for the whole song. I kept the beat. I heard the lyrics. I felt the rhythm and kept it up. I danced. The whole song. I made it through the song. If you can get through the song, you can get through your pain.

So, I'm meant to get through this. But I feel that now I am...slipping. Away. I feel a shift. Like I am losing. Maybe that's the it that I have to get through. Maybe my it wasn't cancer. Maybe my it wasn't fighting but learning to stop, to accept, to let it be. Maybe my it is to embrace my fate. To receive it? Gracefully? Well I plan to die kicking and screaming. I want to leave this earth clutching at it with all my might. I want to chase my last breath and stuff it back down my throat. Is that graceful, Diary? I got through the song, but for the first time, I don't think that is going to translate to my life. I need to accept that I won't get through this. But man, I will fight until the very end.

Dear Diary,

Thursday today. They are really struggling to get my blood. It took six tries this morning; twice in my left arm, once in my right, twice in my bloody foot. I feel my tummy turn over as I write that. They finally got it when they tried my right arm again. Well, Nurse No Name didn't; she had to go get help after her fifth attempt. Rochelle was her help. She got it on the first try. Rochelle told me her name. Perhaps that should be mentioned in your next work appraisal, Nurse No Name.

I have been listening to music nearly all day. Mum went home just as I got my breakfast and she has a few errands to run, so she has the day off today and Evie is staying tonight. I felt that she needed the day off. She looks tired. It's a tough gig to wait out the end with someone.

From a purely selfish point of view, I don't like being on my own in here. I like being on my own in my every-day life but in hospital it's almost scary. I feel like a child afraid to go to sleep without Dad first checking the wardrobe for serial killers.

Roxette and The Bangles have featured heavily on my playlist today. Plus a few random Top 40 style hits. Bruno Mars is telling me that he loves me just the way I am at the moment. Music lifts me up and helps me feel more like me. The real me. Me minus cancer.

One of my biggest pet peeves is people who think they are better than you because of the type of music they listen to. I don't really have a favourite genre. I just like songs that make me feel alive. Ironically (insert laughing emoji here). I love the girl groups from the sixties like The Shangri-Las and I love Russell Morris. But I also love the eighties and if you want to crank a nineties boy band like Backstreet Boys, I'm okay with that. It's amazing how fickle life is. How quickly it can end. How irreversible that loss is. So whatever music you like, who gives a shit as long as it makes you feel something.

I miss Oakley. He hasn't answered any of my messages and Evie said she hasn't heard from him either. She tried to reassure me that he has taken on a few private catering jobs outside of the hotel so he is pretty busy. Luke is meant to be coming in sometime today or tomorrow so I intend to press him for information. Not that Oakley would ever talk to anyone about anything personal. Which is my fault, I know.

My tongue feels bizarrely furry. I keep drinking water like Dr Young told me to, but it honestly feels furry. And my gums feel cold. Like they have their own temperature going on, independent from the rest of my body.

Hope that helps with everyone's exciting research. What an opportunity.

Dear Diary,

I cried in front of Mum today and now I feel like shit. They took some more swabs and stuff and it was nothing I am not used to but I cried. I cried and asked Mum to hold my hand. She was crying herself but tried to hide it from me by talking about Dad and having to pick up his Chinese on the way home and how she must remember to go to the post office this week to pay the electricity bill. I focussed on every word she said as if it was my lifeline.

My arm was sore and the more they tried to pull my blood out the sicker I felt. Like sick to my stomach. I could feel them digging. I was sure if I looked, I would see my bones sticking out of my forearm. I just cried. I wanted to go home and I wanted to watch Welcome to 18. I just cried.

Mum has left for the day and she will break down as soon as she gets in the car. And then again when she gets home. And it's probably the worst feeling in the world to know that.

Evie is here now, chatting to a client on the phone. I asked her if she had heard from Oakley. She said he came over once during the week to pick some things up but he was in a bad mood so she just left him to it. Oh, and that she had seen him stepping out of the elevator when she got to the hospital today!! I can only imagine how pale I must have looked because she asked me, "Didn't he come to see you today? He was walking out the hospital as I was walking in." I told her I must have been asleep. Well I have been awake all day, as unusual as that is for me. So, what the hell is going on there? He comes in to see me, changes his mind and leaves?

Is he that mad at me that he can't even see me? Losing my life and my best friend too it would seem.

My brain feels ten seconds behind everyone else's. I think the cancer is inducing early signs of dementia. I have a throbbing headache. And my eyeballs hurt. It's more like a migraine. I'm going to have a sleep now.

I am sick of today.

I hope I dream about my red dress and all that it used to entail.

Even though some people obviously don't like red dresses any more.

The seventh chapter

Luke placed a cooler bag on my tray table. I smiled from ear to ear as I instinctively prepared my taste buds for one of his infamous milkshakes.

"You have no idea how much I have been missing these!"

"I suspected as much, so it's double chocolate."

Luke pulled a chair closer to the bed, while I relished my first mouthful of his coveted milkshake. He was wearing a particularly smart looking suit today; tailored to a perfect fit of course. He has always been the proper grown-up in our group.

"How weird is it at home with just you and Eves?" I asked between obnoxiously large gulps. "Do you feel like a married couple?"

"Well it's funny you should mention that actually." Luke took off his suit jacket and slung it over the back of his chair. "Evie met Annabelle."

I dropped my mouth open dramatically and Luke chuckled.

"By accident, of course. She stayed over at our house the other day, just because we got back from the concert pretty late. I was just going to nip in and get my stuff for work the next day, then go back to her house, but Evie was already asleep in her room. Honestly, I felt like I was a 16-year-old kid, scared Mum and Dad would wake up and find out I was sneaking in my girlfriend. I walked her out in the morning and Evie was already up having her coffee. Like seriously, when have you ever known Evie to get up before seven? The one time she does, hey."

"Far out! You must have shit yourself!" I laughed. "Was Evie a bitch to her?"

Luke contemplated his answer, mentally searching for the right adjective.

"She was polite. But Annabelle gave me the silent treatment as I drove her home. She said I should have told her how stunning Evie was." Luke rolled his eyes. "Same old story."

Luke said he spent the entire drive reassuring Annabelle that he doesn't think of Evie as anything more than a friend.

"To be honest it would have been easier if she didn't believe me and wanted to break up, cos now she's always going to be paranoid of her. Like my girlfriends always are."

"So, she's totally fine with the fact that you live with a beautiful, strong, confident woman who you've been lusting after since high school?"

"Yep." Luke actually looked disappointed. "She thinks I must not notice how beautiful Evie is and reckons that's a sign that I only have eyes for her." He slumped back dramatically in his chair. "I feel like the next few weeks will be hell now."

"I'm impressed you let one of your girlfriends meet her, even if it was by accident. You never bring your girlfriends around."

"I mean, it's not a conscious decision not to, I just never really think to bring them over. I don't know. It wasn't planned. I thought Evie would be out with her new loser and I only intended to shoot through to pick up my stuff. You know, I mean Evie is so beautiful and most girls don't like that. If they see how gorgeous my best friend is, they get paranoid. Remember Susie? She'd interrogate me every time Evie sent me a message and even asked me to delete the photos I had of Evie on my phone. Plus, I love your sister, but she's a bitch. She picks my girlfriends to bits and makes me feel like I should be embarrassed by them. Remember Beth? Evie said she dressed like a Mormon. Remember Lily? Evie asked me if she was 'actually sixty five.' Remember Yasmina? Evie so kindly offered to take her shopping and give her a make-over, should she ever decide to 'start making an effort with her appearance.' Remember Jane?"

I laughed and put my hand over his mouth. "I get it! And geez, how many girlfriends have you had, dude?"

"Probs like thirty because your sister hates them all!"

I missed Luke's company the second he went home and was grateful to see Dad arrive shortly after.

"Eat, you're looking so thin, darling."

Dad buttered my toast right to the corners and cut it into halves. I merrily tucked into the scrambled eggs while Dad eagerly told me how Yesterday by The Beatles originally included the lyric, 'scrambled eggs, oh, my baby, how I love your legs.' Yesterday was first released on A Collection of Beatles Oldies, in December 1966. I know this because Dad told me as I ate my lunch. I hadn't wanted any of my breakfast this morning as I was feeling too nauseous. I was disappointed because I love breakfast food the most, so I was grateful when the kitchen prepared a surprise 'breakfast lunch' for me.

By the time I got to my cereal, I could tell you Yesterday's producer, track listing and even name the B-side. Act Naturally, in case you were wondering.

Dad exuded a level of comfort and security that was unparalleled. I wanted to record his voice so I could play it every night as I fell asleep. I wanted to capture one of his hugs in a glass jar and release it any time I felt like the world was escaping me.

"We caught up with The Lawsons last night. Pompous arse that Mitch has become. Your mother didn't do a good job of pretending, as you'd expect."

"No, when Mum doesn't like someone it's pretty obvious."

"Got that right. She was most unfriendly. Have to have a word with her about that."

"Have a word with me about what?" Dad and I turned to the door to see Mum arriving from her sandwich hunt.

"You, being unfriendly towards The Lawsons." Dad raised his eyebrows.

"Pompous arse, he is. And she's no better."

Mum kissed my forehead and placed her handbag on the bedside table. I looked back to the door to see if she had left her overnight bag there, but she just had her handbag.

"Are you not staying tonight, Mum?"

"No, dear but you won't be on your own. It's all been co-ordinated."

I took that to mean Evie was going to be my roommate again, which surprised me as she told me she had a date.

"Quite an honour to have Evie give up one of her date nights for me," I said in surprise.

Mum smiled and sat down next to Dad. They bickered over Mum's apparent 'obvious' attitude in front of the Lawsons and Mum shared half her chicken salad roll with Dad.

"Not bad, is it?" Mum asked as she bit into her half.

Dad sampled another, larger mouthful before declaring, "Not bad at all!"

Do you ever catch yourself in a moment? As if you are looking in on yourself, watching your life, from the window outside? Acting in your own movie. I do. All the time. I script conversations in my head before releasing them into social reality. I compile soundtracks. I edit scenes later in my head. Wouldn't life be amazing if it really was like that? Really like a movie? Slow motion scenes, empowering music, happy endings. Maybe it's just easier for me to pretend that this isn't real life. That I am just watching a movie and not feeling myself die. I am a therapist's dream.

I watched Mum and Dad as if watching an episode of my favourite T.V. show. We could have just as easily been sitting in a lounge room or at a restaurant. My current mis en scene is depressing as shit. The hospital bed should be a patio chair. I can see it. We are sitting outside. No machines beeping. No call bells. No hand sanitizers affixed to the walls. I can actually feel it. Movies are powerful like that.

I thrived off of Mum and Dad's mundane conversation about Dad's latest inconsiderate customer, about Mum's worry over Evie getting too down about Ryan and the fact that they must remember to buy toilet paper on the way home. I think 'mundane' is my most favourite word ever. It encompasses everything that breaks my heart about being forced to leave this life before I am ready.

"Knock, knock!"

I swiftly looked to the door and inhaled louder than I intended when I saw who was standing there.

"Miss me?" Oakley was wearing black jeans and a white shirt, rolled up to his elbows. The first three buttons were undone. He was a movie star. In that moment I cursed the universe for not letting me be his leading lady.

I stood up with Mum and Dad and they hugged him as he approached. Mum pulled his shirt together at the collar to conceal his chest. He tilted his head and smiled.

"Thanks, Mum but you're ruining my sex appeal."

"Time for us oldies to leave you two kids to it!" Dad wrapped his arms around me tightly and Mum did the same.

I frowned in confusion and Mum said, "He buzzed you for the weekend. Evie gave me strict instructions not to object."

Oakley smiled a smile that was just meant for me and I was so excited I had to restrain myself from slapping my hands together like a seal thanking its keeper for the fish.

Mum and Dad left the room hand in hand and closed the door behind them. I was beaming.

"I thought you hated me?" I babbled.

Oakley dropped his two bags by the bed and stated matter-of-factly, "No, I love you. And I understand, even if it kills me. I would rather be your friend than your nothing. I needed some time. I came to see you every day."

"What? When?" I was simultaneously furious and relieved.

"Every day. I watched you from the top of the corridor. You can see straight in here from the elevator."

"Why didn't you come in instead of stalking me like a serial killer? Why didn't you want to see me?"

He lifted my hand into his and held it by my side. "I saw you. Every day. But I just couldn't bring myself to see you. Does that make sense?"

"Yep," I admitted to him and myself, "it does."

Our gaze was intense and my eyes pleaded for him to kiss me. But my heart knew I would only hurt him again, and the look on his face told me that he knew that, too.

"I'm so sorry about all of this, Oakley. I have messed you around so many times. I was never trying to hurt you. I just- "

"Yeah, I get it." He spoke softly and sincerely. "I almost wish I didn't so that I could hate you, but I get it."

I walked over to the window and pulled the curtains back to reveal the glorious afternoon sun. Oakley came to stand behind me and rested his head on my shoulder. I smiled shyly.

"Your kind of weather, Mack. The sun shines just for you, I'm certain."

My skin tingled and a warmth filled my soul. His hand slipped to my thigh and playfully tugged at my track suit pants.

"The sun shines just for you and you mock it with these bloody things!"

I playfully pushed my bottom back into him to push him away and giggled uncontrollably. Oakley giggled too and it sounded heavenly.

He picked up his two bags from the floor and chucked them on the bed. Shifting the smaller of the two to one side, he patted it and explained, "this one has my undies and toothbrush in it, and all the other stuff I need to keep up my rugged good looks."

He pulled the green duffle bag towards him and unzipped it, releasing a handful of DVDs, women's gossip magazines and Scrabble.

"This bag, this one has us in it. You up for a match?"

It was an intense game. We lay facing each other on our tummies, separated by the Scrabble board, laying on top of the standard white hospital blanket and pillows on the floor. It was like our own Scrabble Fort. The scores were almost even. It was my turn. It had been my turn for some time now.

"The best things in life never change," Oakley smirked as he rearranged the letters in his rack.

"Meaning?" I raised my eyebrows.

"You have never taken a turn in less than fifteen minutes. It's one of my favourite things about you."

I laughed. "Surely that would be annoying?"

"No. It's like you want to be so certain. You don't want to regret your decision. You want to know exactly what you are getting yourself in for before you commit...to a word. You take the game seriously."

I was embarrassed by the analogy he was alluding to. I summoned some of Evie's self-confidence and played along with his banter.

"It's not just my words on the board. I'm playing with your words, too."

Oakley smiled to himself and continued to rearrange the letters on his rack. "Touché, m'lady."

I picked up my A and placed it underneath his L. At that moment I wished I had been clever and prepared a word that meant something like 'if only' or 'what if.' Some sort of obvious secret message. Something that told him that I didn't want things to be this way but truly thought there was no other way they could be. But using up all the letters in my rack to spell LANGUISH felt pretty good, too.

"That's a bingo, buddy!"

"Wrong game, smart arse," he smirked in reply.

Oakley instantly put down his letters on the board whilst I picked up my seven new tiles.

"You're too quick!" I grumpily declared. "If you took longer to make your word, then my turn wouldn't have to take so long! You've made it my turn already and I haven't even picked up all my tiles yet!"

"That's not the reason you take so long on your turns, Mack."

"Well you're just going to have to wait."

I positioned my letters on my rack and concentrated on the formation of my next turn. I ignored Oakley's sniggers as my lips silently read through the various possibilities.

"I'm going to time you." Oakley theatrically held his non-existent watch up to his face. "Twelve minutes, thirteen minutes…"

"Lol very funny. Ssh now. Genius at work."

I studied the letters in front of me. Three Is, two Us, a B and a K. I surveyed the board for a decent opening that would enable me to use my B and K but spaces were limited at this point in the game. I sighed in defeat and placed my U and B next to the H that I had so smugly used for LANGUISH only minutes before.

Oakley raised an eyebrow. "Didn't even make double digits on that one, Mack. That could have cost you the game."

"Why, what's the score?" I panicked.

Oakley picked up the tattered, faded black A4-sized notebook from the floor next to him and opened up to one of the last pages. We had been using the same scorebook since our first game eight years ago. There were only a few pages left now and the irony stabbed me in the heart.

I wondered what Oakley would do with the notebook and our Scrabble game after I was gone. Would he keep it? Op shop it? Store it away in a cupboard, only for his grandkids to come across it when they clear out the possessions from his house after ninety-year-old Oakley moves into a nursing home? And then that one little word, that one little thought, grandkids, spiralled everything out of control.

Oakley was going to have grandkids. Of course. Which meant that he was going to have kids. Of course. Which meant that he would find someone to share his life with. Of course. Of course he was going to. Why haven't I realised this, thought about this? Isn't that what I want for him? To live? To have a life? Isn't that why I push him away all the time? Because he can't have one with me? What is he even going to look like when he is ninety? Will his hair still grow at the speed of light? What about in ten years? Will he still be wearing his Degrassi top when he is forty, long after I have gone? Do you hold onto those things, or do you let them go with the person? Shit. My heart aches. Is he still going to be working at the hotel, or will he finally have his own restaurant like he has always dreamed about?

I don't get to see what Oakley's life will be like. Can I just quickly fast forward? I want to see his whole life. I want, need, to know he will be happy. I want to know all the little details that we just take for granted in everyday life. Is he going to go grey or after a lifetime of not being able to keep up with haircuts, will he ironically go bald? Will he keep watching Degrassi on Saturday nights or does tradition die with me…

Bloody hell. I wiped my forehead and felt the sweat moisten my hand. It is so hot in here. My breath quickened and my body temperature soared. I tugged at the collar of my singlet top and stretched it away from my skin.

Oakley read from the score book. "Its two hundred and seventy-six to two hundred and seventy-four. You're the latter. Two points in it."

Oakley smiled but his face changed in an instant when he looked up at me. He abruptly reached across the board and grabbed hold of my hand. "Are you okay? You look like you're going to faint."

"I'm okay. I just need a drink of water, please."

Oakley jumped off the floor, grabbed the glass of water from the bedside table and thrust it in my hand before I had even finished asking for it.

"Should I get the nurse?"

"I'm okay. Honestly. I was just thinking about how much I'm going to miss playing Scrabble with you."

Oakley sighed and pressed his forehead against mine. "I know you don't want to hurt me so I won't tell you how much I'm going to miss this, too."

I exhaled slowly, wanting to breathe in this moment, and Oakley. "It's your turn."

Oakley kissed my cheek and lowered himself back down on his spot on the other side of the board. He studied his letters for much longer than his usual twenty or thirty seconds.

"Now who's taking forever?"

"Well there's only eight tiles left after this turn. And for once I intend to succeed on my plan to win."

Oakley studied the letters in his rack and I studied him. He ran his fingers through his hair and rearranged his letters one more time before placing the first letter on the board.

"How about we make this game a bit more interesting?" He tilted his head and caught my eyes with his.

I bit my lip in anticipation. His eyes lit up and he continued to place his letters on the board without breaking his gaze. My mouth opened as I mentally added up his score; twenty-eight points for PRIZED. Oakley smiled a ridiculously sexy smile and I scrunched my nose to the side.

"Interesting how? I need to know the specifics before I commit to anything."

Oakley chuckled at my anxiety. "My Mackenzie, you're not a gambler, are you?"

I love the way he speaks to me, the way he always finds a way to insert a little pet name or some hint of affection. He threw his head back and laughed at my anxious expression. "You know you'll end up winning, you always do. So, what are you scared of?"

I breathed out my nerves. "Okay. What do I have to do if you win?"

"Have a shower with me tonight."

I rolled my eyes and giggled against my will. "You're such a sixteen-year-old boy. What if I win?"

"State your terms."

My eyes widened with potential. I bit my lip and smiled from the inside out.

"The possibilities are endless. I like having this power!"

Oakley chuckled into his chest. "Be nice to me."

I looked around the room for inspiration. My attention focussed on his faded denim jacket swung over the bed.

"If I win, I get to keep your jacket."

"You can have anything of mine you want. Anything, any time. You don't need to win a bet for that."

I wanted to leap across the Scrabble board and wrap my whole body around him. I didn't deserve to have someone as amazing as Oakley in my life.

My ears pricked up at the sounds around me; a woman coughing up a lung in the room next door. Machines beeping. Call bells ringing. Nurses feet shuffling. I looked at the butterfly needle tapped to my hand.

"If it wasn't for the cancer, I would have everything I could ever want because of you. I only want to live, and that's largely because of you, too."

I spoke softly and stared at the ground. I wanted to see Oakley's reaction but I was afraid to look at him.

"I pull away every time because it hurts to love you back. When you know you are going to die, to feel every second of every day, what you are going to lose, it crushes you. But even though I push you away, you make me feel like you will always come back."

I exhaled deeply and swallowed down my tears. "So that's all I would want to win: my life. I love it. And you go hand in hand with all of that. I am losing that particular game, the game of life. Just like every single person in this ward. But I can win this game, the game of Scrabble. And if I do, I want everyone in this ward to win with me. If I win, you have to go for a slow stroll around the ward. No clothes allowed."

Oakley burst into laughter. "What the fuck, are you serious?"

"A slow walk! Around the whole ward! And no cupping your hands anywhere! Give that lady next door something to smile about. Give that guy down the corridor a laugh. Make the nurses forget that they watch people die every day. Do we have a bet?"

Oakley tilted his head and raised his eyebrows. I think he was impressed. "We have a bet, Mackenzie. But you realise you are currently losing by twelve points?"

"I'll win," I nodded my head confidently.

I shuffled my letters around and concentrated on behalf of the nurse who was working her second double shift in a row, on behalf of the nineteen year old girl in room four who was recovering from her second lung biopsy in three years, on behalf of the forty two year old Dad with stage four bowel cancer down the hall who sobbed for hours every night after his kids left. And I concentrated for the thirty-year-old girl who had no idea who she even was anymore, independent of cancer.

Much quicker than usual, I picked up my letters and placed them on the board.

"Twenty-seven, not bad at this point in the game. I think that's a record for your quickest turn ever."

I assured him, "I want to win."

Oakley took his turn almost straight away, scoring nine points towards his total. I had two tiles left, he had five.

I played ON for two points.

He used his blank to spell IF for one point.

I pressed my lips together to contain my excitement. I needed seven points to be victorious. I had an I. But I had a secret weapon in my possession; the S. I gleefully scanned through the words on the board and mentally added up every single one to see which would be worth the most if I pluralised it.

I picked up my two letters, caught Oakley's stare, and placed them down, smiling at his mortification the whole time. I turned CHIP into CHIPS. Oakley's face became void of all signs of life.

"Fuck me," he breathed, "you won." If there was a doctor present in the room, they would have surely diagnosed him with shock.

I could not contain my laughter. "At least it's a warm day!"

Oakley rubbed his hands along his knees, quietly chanting "oh fuck" repeatedly into the ceiling. I collapsed onto my side and lay on the floor holding my tummy. My ribs ached from laughing and I just could not stop.

"Fucking hell!" Oakley found himself laughing along with me, much to his surprise.

A knock at the door quietened the moment and a nurse entered with her med trolley. Seconds later my tummy was rattling with its feast of tablets and medicine. If I was a cartoon, I could shake myself like a maraca.

The nurse left the room and Oakley stared at the empty pill cup. Motivation struck him.

"Alright, fuck it. Let's go, penis."

He stood from the Scrabble board and hastily pulled his top over his head. He was bare foot so merely unzipped his jeans and let them slide effortlessly over his feet. He stood before me in his briefs with his hands on his hips.

"Are you waiting for me to tell you that you don't have to do this? Because I am having the most fun!" I giggled at his misery.

"I know you are, that's why they're coming off!" Oakley swiftly dropped his jocks and stood before me in all his glory. My whole face smiled and I cheered as his pasty white butt cheeks headed towards the door.

Outside my room, the ward was disappointingly empty. Oakley walked calmly and slowly down the corridor towards the lift. There was not one soul around to witness his naked parade and my shoulders slumped in disappointment. He neared the nurses' station at the end of the corridor, just as the lift made a loud ping.

"Oh fuck, here we go," Oakley announced to himself.

The doors to the lift slid apart to reveal an elderly woman, holding on to an intravenous pole. The tubing crept under her night dress and the husband was just finishing fussing over it as the doors opened.

The elderly gentleman stepped out of the lift first, reaching his hand back to hold onto his wife's free hand. He looked forward and caught sight of Oakley, instantly exclaiming "What in the world? Cover your eyes, Maude!" Maude shrieked in delight and her husband quickly shot his hands up to shield her eyes. Maude just as quickly moved her head to the side for a better view.

"Evening, ma'am," Oakley nodded politely and proceeded to turn the corner at the nurses' station.

Maude's smile made me glow with happiness. She was right chuffed with herself.

Standing in my doorway, I was instantly aware of the squeals sounding from the nurses' station. I could no longer see Oakley but could hear the nurses and doctors cheering, clapping, laughing and screaming. The sounds alone made for an amazing atmosphere, exactly like I had hoped for.

The patients all rushed to their doorways to see what was going on. Oakley turned the other corner of the square ward and started his slow stroll back to my room. The woman next door, who I only ever hear cough, stood at her door grinning from ear to ear. Her tears of laughter gave me goose bumps and I found myself watching her more than the perfect naked man walking towards me. The father down the hall took photos on his phone and gleefully called out, "I'm sending these to the Missus!" Oakley was calm all the while, posing for selfies with the nurses and high fiving patients as they all took their turns to gawk.

His parade around the layout of the ward created so much noise I was paranoid an alarm would go off. The clapping, whistling, cheering and promises to make him "go viral" were so energetic and full of life, surely we all forgot how much death surrounded us.

Mere steps from my room, Oakley's eyes found mine, waiting for him like an excited fan at a meet and greet. His face erupted into a smile and he pursed his lips like a sixteen-year-old girl taking mirror selfies. Even in the midst of humiliation, he still tries to make me laugh.

When he reached my room, I bit my bottom lip and shook my head in amazement. Oakley turned his back on me, waved to his cheering fans, thanked them for their support like the true gentleman he is, and then ever so coolly strolled on in, closed the door behind him, and hastily put on his clothes.

"Fucking Scrabble!" he laughed as he did.

The Ninth Chapter

Dear Diary,

I am having my new thing implanted in my vein today. I feel tired. Awake. Anxious. Calm. Nervous. Excited. Scared. I'm scared.

If only I could wear my trackies during the operation.

Being put to sleep scares me. Big time. I worry that I don't have enough energy in me to wake up again.

If I don't, have I said everything I need to say? I haven't done everything. Nowhere near it. But saying things is different to doing things. Have I said it all? Have I told everyone what I need to say? Does Mum know that I fight for her? Does Dad know that he is my safe place? Does Evie know that she is my rock? Does Luke know that his milkshakes make me feel loved? Does Oakley know, just know? Geez. This is starting to sound more like a suicide note than a diary entry.

The orderly arrived and is now pushing me in my bed down to the theatre. He looks like that dude from Clueless and Can't Hardly Wait. What is his name? Ah man, that's going to drive me bonkers. And Rat Race! He was in that, too. Brian? Brandon? It was a B, definitely a B. Shit, what was his name?

Well he's going to take you back to my room, Diary. I asked him and he said "absolutely, I can do that for you, easy." Nice guy. Barry? Nah. Baxter?

I think I'm going to miss you, Gold Flecks. It's unexpectedly helpful writing in you. I hope I wake up and can write in you more.

I forgot to tell you, that's your name. Gold Flecks. I hope you like it. It suits you.

Hello Gold Flecks!

It's Monday. I think the surgery was yesterday. Or today it was Wednesday. I had some custard and it was pink. Or medicine. I thought it was custard at the time but now maybe not. I think Bailey brought you back to the room.

Dear Diary,

Friggin lol. It's Wednesday today. I don't even remember writing that last entry and I certainly don't recall eating pink custard or medicine. Hilarious. Never give pen and paper to someone coming out of anaesthetic.

I'm told everything went really well. I am still in bed. I feel very weak and sore. My skin is a bit tingly and my arm aches where the implant is. Mum and Dad are here. They are cuddled up together on the couch. Mum is doing her crossword book and Dad is reading a biography on George Harrison. I got off the phone with Evie just before; she is going out on a date Friday night with some guy she met at the gym. He works at Sanity. His name is Jayy. I'm not sure why two Ys are warranted but there you go.

They just bought my lunch in. Going to try to eat something because they tell me I have to but I really don't have any appetite at all. How weird is that; I'm normally famished 24/7.

Dear Gold Flecks,

Thursday used to be my favourite day, back when I was working. It was delivery day at work so I would spend the afternoon unpacking the continence aids and stacking them in the pad room. Like real life Tetris. I YouTubed songs on my phone and had the room so organised that it made the carers feel excited when they had to come in to get a spare pad. Well, I hoped so anyway.

I miss working. I haven't been able to work much since I was diagnosed. I tried for the first few months but generally had to call in sick for the majority of my shifts, which wasn't fair on the home. I joined an agency for a couple of years so that I could work when I felt up to it. I usually managed to work the weekend so that certainly helped Mum and Dad out with me, financially. It's been about three years now since my last shift. I miss working. Cancer really does take everything away from you.

So instead of spending my Thursday grouping the pads by size, I am here. They've connected a drip to my new implant and I'm getting my usual cocktail of shit pumped into me. This room is far grander than the dingy pad room but being in it certainly doesn't bestow me with the same sense of fulfillment or pride.

I don't even know why I'm thinking about all that stuff. Maybe I'm just trying to clutch onto the life I have/had in a vain attempt to make my body fight harder. I don't even know if that makes any sense outside of my head, on your pages. At some point I know I will accept my fate, as psychology dictates. It is coming around far faster than I want it to. I just can't ever imagine being at peace with it. I can't imagine being okay with never getting to stock up a pad room again.

I am being discharged tomorrow. And you are coming with me, Gold Flecks. Dr Young told me to keep writing in you for as long as I can. I like writing in you. It's helping me, not them. Deep down, I think that was Dr Young's intention all along.

Hey Gold Flecks,

I'm all packed and I'm ready to go home! Mum is at the nurses' station signing some paperwork and Dad has taken my bags down to the car. It's boiling today. Dad said it's meant to get to 42. It's 10am and it's already 37. Days like this I wish I had never got into the rut of wearing my trackies. I have a t-shirt on but my thighs are sweating so much I probably look like I have peed myself.

Evie has her date tonight and I keep reminding myself every few minutes, like literally saying 'Evie, date' in my head so I don't forget. I forget so many things. It's a conscious effort to not throw up all day so I guess there's not much mental room left for anything else.

As excited and relieved as I am to be going home, I am nervous. How crazy is that. Here, there are nurses and doctors all around me. It has been so freeing to just be the patient. When I'm home, I exhaust myself trying to get through the day as if I am not sick. When I'm home, it is a conscious effort to be Mack. I hate to admit it but I needed to not be Mack for a little while. I needed this rest. I needed to be the patient.

Oh, and I Googled it: his name is Breckin Meyer.

The Tenth Chapter

Evie slid the pamphlet across the kitchen table. "We're doing this! One more month, and we are doing this!"

I studied the woman on the front. She looked like she was probably around my age. Her grin spread across her face like a half moon in the night sky; so prominent and captivating. She was plummeting towards the earth, towards her possible death, yet I have never seen a human look so free.

TRY THE SKY was written in bold red letters, stretched across the pamphlet. I found the decision to use red lettering an odd one but maybe not everyone makes the correlation between red and blood.

"Red for the blood splattering from your dead body," Oakley spoke nonchalantly, remaining engrossed in the New Weekly magazine. I smiled to myself and prayed he wasn't able to hear any more of my thoughts.

"Hey! How come I didn't get a flake?" Evie swiped her finger across the top of her milkshake, scooping up the whipped cream and placing it in her mouth.

Luke mumbled to himself and went back to the bench to get another flake out of the packet. He rolled his eyes as he placed it atop Evie's milkshake.

"Happy?" He seemed to be in a bad mood this morning and a little less tolerant of Evie's princess demands. I wondered if it had anything to do with the fact that Evie stayed out to two a.m. on her date with Jayy with two Ys last night.

Evie smiled like a five-year-old who had just been told her public tantrum worked and her mum was going to buy her that toy after all.

Luke sat on the bar stool on the other side of the table and we all dived in to our milkshakes. Cue music; Merril Bainbridge, Under the Water. We must have looked like we were on a commercial; all merrily sitting around with milkshakes, revelling in each other's company, and me sitting there with love heart eyes for them all. I took in each of their faces, listening to the sweet melody of Merril as Evie blabbed on about the annoying man she sits next to at work and Oakley reminding me to "actually take" the pot of tablets sitting next to me. The movie camera in my head panned across the table and rested on each of their eyes, on their mouths, and then back to me, adoring them all.

"I mean it, Mack, actually take the tablets. Don't just let them sit there," Oakley insisted.

"Yes, Doctor Bains." I picked up the pill pot and tipped the plethora of tablets down my throat, washing it down with a big gulp of my milkshake. "Happy?" I smiled, not meaning to sound like Evie.

"No, but satisfied," Oakley firmly stated.

"Anyone up for a movie tonight?" Luke asked as he flipped the pages of the paper.

"I'm out with Jayy," Evie quickly informed him.

"Second date the very next day? Bit much, don't you think?" Luke seemed genuinely annoyed.

"No," Evie replied, just as annoyed, "just means he likes me. Is that so hard to believe?"

"Not at all, but you don't even know this guy with two ys and you're going to spend your whole weekend with him?"

"Are you serious? You're actually going to make fun of his name? What are you, like twelve now?" Evie was worked up and I began to feel nervous in anticipation of the impending eruption.

"Well that would match the emotional maturity of most of the guys with two ys that you date!" Luke raised his voice to match Evie's.

"Yeah you're probably right. I should get myself a nice little uptight, controlling type with the personality of a sock who only ever wants to socialise with their own friends and doesn't have anything at all to do with my life!"

"Oh please, you've met Annabelle literally once."

"Yeah, because you never bring her over! You hide her! Or do you hide us?"

"You couldn't hide Jayy even if you wanted to, which you should want to, by the way, considering you're a grown arse woman and he looks like he just flunked out of Summer Bay High. For an intelligent woman, you sure you do make stupid decisions when it comes to who you let into your bed! But even if you tried, how on earth could you hide a man with a bun the size of an exercise ball on the top of his head?"

"I don't want to hide my boyfriends! My boyfriends are all fucking hot and the sex is fucking amazing! Tell us, Luke, why do you hide your girlfriends, hey? Embarrassed because they're all insecure frumps?"

Evie and Luke stared intensely at each other with their words lingering in the air around us. Oakley looked at me uncomfortably and I took a big sip of my milkshake. Evie wanted Luke to retaliate but he just shook his head and narrowed his eyes.

"You know what," Evie slid out from the spot on the bench next to me, "fuck this! I do not need this from you! You're just being an asshole, Luke. You are frustrated with your own dull and lifeless relationships and taking it out on me! Fuck that and fuck you, okay?"

Luke pushed his stool back and stood up opposite her. "And you're just being a bitch because you're embarrassed your boyfriend doesn't know how to spell his own goddamn name! On behalf of intelligent people everywhere, Jay has one y!"

Evie rolled her eyes and stormed off to her room, slamming the door behind her. Luke pressed his lips together and mumbled "fuck!" as he slammed his fist into the table and left the kitchen. Seconds later, the front door closed and Luke's car revved its engine before loudly pulling out of the drive way.

I took another sip of my milkshake and Oakley did the same. We drank the rest in silence.

I carefully picked up the paper Luke had left on the table and started reading all the bad news the world had to offer today. Oakley whispered that he needed to borrow my phone, so he played around with it for a minute or so and then basically tiptoed to the sink to do some washing up. He picked up each spoon, glass and plate with such care that not a single clang could be heard. Noticing his attempt to not make a sound made me aware that I had been turning each page as if it was on the verge of breaking.

"I'm going to get going for a bit," Oakley whispered face to face. "I'm taking Mum and Dad out for an early tea but I'll shoot by afterwards for a movie, yeah? Teen Witch?"

"Have a good time. Actually, we're overdue for Girls Just Want to Have Fun," I whispered back. "Why are we being so quiet?"

"Probably because that was terrifying," he smiled.

His smile induced my own. "See you later."

Oakley left and I went to my room for a lie down. The aftershock of Evie and Luke's earthquake had rattled me. They had never had a fight before, much less in front of us all.

The doctors always say that the timeframe they give me is just an approximate. But what if they were being generous or misjudged it? What if it's not months left but days? Hours? What if I die while Luke and Evie are still fighting?

There's this sense of urgency that comes with knowing your own doom, of living with a deadline. I don't watch new series in case I don't get the chance to finish them. I keep my room meticulously clean and tidy knowing that Evie will come in after I am gone. I keep unnecessary possessions to a minimum so I don't leave anyone with the burden of holding onto trinkets that only make them sad. And I try so hard to keep the peace.

I haven't gone in to Evie's room and I know she is expecting me to. I don't want to fight with her. I can't. And if I go in there, I know we would. She is worked up, and for the most part, I agree with everything Luke said.

If I go in there and we fight and then I die before we make up, Evie will feel like shit for the rest of her life. I constantly think about the way someone feels around me, like I don't just consider it, I obsess over it. I never want to leave anyone feeling anything other than happy. Or loved. Or appreciated. Or valued. Because it could literally be the last memory they will have of me. It's ironic that dying teaches us how to live.

So, I don't want to fight with Evie and when she gets in this mood, she will pick a fight with absolutely anyone and everyone. If an ant crossed her path she would crouch down to its level and shout "what the hell is your problem?" at the poor bugger.

I came to my room to rest but it feels more like I am hiding. I have my T.V on mute and I'm scrolling through Facebook on my phone. I'm actually scared that she'll come looking for me. I'm hoping she'll see the house is quiet and just assume everyone went out. It's five o'clock so she'll be going out with Jayy soonish anyway.

Just as I think this, I hear Evie's bedroom door click open. I quieten my breath and quickly turn off the T.V so that the light doesn't draw her attention to my room. I wait. Silence.

It's almost comical, sitting here, barely breathing, so that my volatile sister doesn't come looking for a fight, on the off chance that I might die before we make up. I listen to her footsteps. She is in the bathroom taking a wee which means she will be leaving pretty much straight after. I'm relieved; taking shallow breaths is not easy when you are running on near zero energy.

The sink is running water and then the bathroom door closes. She is in the lounge room now, closing all the curtains by the sounds of it. Then a car honks and I hear her say "great," only half-heartedly, before leaving the house.

When I hear the front door click, I carefully open my door and creep over to the front curtain. I peer through to see a black Commodore gassing up the drive way. A teenage-looking boy I can only assume is Jayy is waiting in the car, hanging his arm low out the window. He looks like a gender fluid model on his way to a poetry reading, who might also engage in a Boyz N the Hood drive-by on the way home. Lady Antebelllum are playing on his car stereo. The dude really needs to settle on a style already.

Evie opened up the door to the front passenger side and I could tell she was glad no one saw. The Evie Mum and Dad raised would have waited for him to knock on the front door instead of running out in answer to his honk.

They drive off and I instantly regret not going into her room so she could pick a fight with me.

"Luke's right, his hair is ridiculous," I utter to myself.

I make myself a salad for tea and sit outside with my book. I had almost read half of it when the alarm on my phone sounded. I reached over to the table to silence it. TAKE YOUR PILLS, my screen read.

"Oakley," I smile and head to the kitchen to down the next batch of pills. I could still feel the last lot rattling around.

A knock at the door broke my self-pity.

"Who is it?" I ask through the wood.

"Lol it's me, Mack."

"Oakley?" I ask in surprise.

He chuckled. "Yes, don't you know my voice? You gonna let me in?"

"Why are you knocking? You never knock. Did you forget your key?"

"I wasn't sure if Evie was still here," he replied in a loud whisper.

I opened the door and met his smile with my own. "The tornado has swept through."

We made our way into the lounge room. Oakley set up the couch with pillows and blankets and I rummaged through our usual pile of DVDs to find Sarah Jessica's best work.

"Did you take the eight o'clock ones?" Oakley pries as he pours our traditional peanut M&Ms into a bowl.

"Just before you got here. You've evidently set up alarms on my phone, I can't forget even if I want to."

I could tell by the smirk on his face that he was pleased with himself.

I put the movie in the DVD player and snuggled in next to Oakley. I was about to press play when the loud clang of keys landing on the kitchen table alerted us to the fact that Luke was home.

"I mean is it just me," he spouted as soon as he stepped into the room, "or is your sister seriously fucked up sometimes?"

"She's passionate," I reasoned.

"No, she's fucking psycho! And she dates losers! What is the appeal? Huh? Someone please explain it to me! Like seriously, explain it to me because it does my head in."

He flopped himself down on the couch next to Oakley.

"I literally do not get it. She's gorgeous, smart, opinionated, feisty, independent, successful, yet every single guy she dates is a moron. Every single guy is a total loser. And I'm a jerk because I see that? Because I see that she deserves better?"

Oakley glared at him uncomfortably. "Sit on the other side, yeah?"

Luke rolled his eyes and dramatically stood up and stepped over Oakley and I, sitting back down next to me.

"What are we watching? Please say it's a shoot em up, beat em up movie. I need someone to get kicked in the face."

"What about Helen Hunt as the best side kick of all time?" I offered.

Luke looked pained and held his tummy. "Please, can we please just watch something with some violence in it? I need violence. Preferably towards a twat with a man bun."

"I'll check what's on," I resigned, picking up the other remote.

Luke tucked his legs under his bottom and rested his head on my shoulder. Oakley did the same on the other side of me. I wish someone was around to take a photo. I felt blissful.

"What about Miss Congeniality?" I asked. Sandra Bullock stared at us from the screen awaiting our decision.

"I need violence, sorry Sandra," Luke spoke to the T.V.

"You need Van Damme," I nodded with certainty.

I got up and grabbed Sudden Death from the DVD cabinet and the boys simultaneously exclaimed "Bingo!" when I pressed play.

We watched the movie, stuffed our bellies full of peanut M&Ms, and Oakley and I shot each other concerned glances over how much joy Luke seemed to derive from watching Van Damme push some dude's face into a meat grinder.

"Good way to chop off a man bun, hey?" he deduced with disturbing glee in his voice.

When the movie finished, Luke sat up and glared at the front window.

"Bit late, isn't it? Shouldn't she be home by now? I mean isn't that rude? She knows you wait up for her and you're sick, you need your rest."

I giggled at his irritation.

"Dude, don't use me as an excuse! It's like ten forty-five. She probably won't be home for an hour or two. And I have no intention of waiting up for her and you shouldn't either. You know as well as I do that she'll just be wanting round two so don't give her the bait."

By the look on Luke's face, I am pretty sure that he was about to agree with me but the unexpected sound of a car pulling into the drive way made us all sit up like meerkats.

"Shit! What do we do?" Luke panicked.

"Hide?" Oakley suggested.

I tapped him on the arm. "She's my sister, remember?"

"She's scary, remember?" he retorted.

"Good point. Hide."

I pointed the remote at the T.V and abruptly turned it off. Luke reached over to the lamp next to him and switched that off, too. Oakley pulled the blanket over our heads. The door clicked open and we slumped down low on the couch like naughty siblings hiding under the table.

Evie chucked her keys on the kitchen table and filled a glass of water from the tap. We heard the glass land rather heavily on the sink and gave each other a knowing look. She was still in a bad mood.

The back of the couch could be seen from the kitchen so we all sunk lower to avoid our blanket heads poking over the top. Evie switched off the kitchen light, loudly mumbling to herself, "yeah sure, just leave everything for me to do," and walked heavy footed down to her room. We heard the door close and looked at each other to see who was going to be the bravest to move first.

"You don't even live here, Oaks," Luke whispered, "you go first."

"Fuck," Oakley chuckled quietly.

We peeled the blanket away slowly and rose from the couch even more slowly. The three of us tip toed to the door and only breathed when we were safely on the other side of it.

"Fresh air!" I quietly joked, clutching at my chest.

Luke and I started walking Oakley to his car, moving painfully slow so as not to set off the sensor light on the front patio.

"I knew I saw your car!" came Evie's roar behind us.

The sensor light came on and we all jumped.

"Where were you all? Where you hiding? Seriously?" Evie's hands were fixated firmly on her hips and her face was scrunched up in a rage. "Afraid I might bring my loser boyfriend in to meet you?"

"Evie," I started.

"No, you can shut up!" Evie snapped. "You are a fine one to comment on any of my boyfriends! You don't even let your boyfriend BE your boyfriend!"

"Evie, calm down," Oakley interjected.

"Oh, fuck off, Oakley! You're not her boyfriend outside of closed doors so don't try to fucking act like it now!"

Luke's face shot to me. "What? What the fuck? Am I drunk? I don't understand a thing that is going on here!"

The sensor light went out and Luke shimmied his body and waved his arms above his head until it came on again.

"Oh!" Evie squealed in delight. "Didn't your bestie tell you?"

"Evie that's enough, mate," Oakley tried to reason with her. "You've had a bad day, you're pissed off at Luke, we get it. I'm going home, everyone else is going to bed. Let's just all calm down."

Evie rolled her eyes. "Always so diplomatic, hey Oaks? Always changing subjects, deflecting attention. You must be as stupid as I am, Luke."

Oakley glared at her. "Evie, that's enough."

Evie smirked and looked to Luke. "So, Oakley hasn't told you then, has he?"

I bowed my head. She was unstoppable.

"Told me what?" Luke asked, feigning disinterest.

The sensor light went out again and Evie jumped back and forth as she spoke, "Told you why he never has a girlfriend longer than one or two weeks here and there?"

The light came on and she stood adamantly with her hands on her hips, leaning her torso in towards Luke.

"Tell me, those times that your best friend does have a girlfriend, is it because you nag him to get one? Because you set him up with someone? Because you tell him to get out there and meet someone? And you're always so stumped when he pulls the plug after one or two dates. Ever get the feeling that he just has a date here and there, like it's a sort of cover?"

Luke looked at Oakley and frowned. "Dude, if you're gay I really don't care."

Evie chuckled. "He's not gay, you oblivious twit! He's been fucking my sister for years."

I stared at my feet and swallowed back the tears.

Luke gasped. "What? Bullshit!" He looked to Oakley and I. "How on earth did I not know this?"

A deafening silence engulfed us and the sensor light went out again. We stood like statues, frozen still in the darkness, waiting for someone else to make a move. Luke finally sighed loudly and repeatedly waved his arms above his head.

"Okay, so fuck it, who cares," he announced.

The sensor light came on and Luke laughed to himself.

"So, two of my best mates are getting it on." He looked at Oakley and I. "You could have told me. I would have been happy for you. But you didn't, so fine, let's get over that. No big deal. Alright. Everyone happy now? Everything out in the open?"

I smiled gratefully and Oakley softly said, "thanks, mate."

This seemed to anger Evie even more.

"WHAT? THAT'S your response?" Evie roared into the night sky. "They've been lying, pretending, sneaking, for YEARS and THAT'S your response? Yet my boyfriend has a man bun and suddenly I'm the only one who makes shit decisions around here?"

"I didn't say it wasn't a shit decision but their decision doesn't affect me!" Luke shouted.

"Oh, and my boyfriends somehow affect you?" she yelled.

"You're damn right they do! Every three to six months, when they inevitably end up cheating on you or going to jail or blowing you off, breaking your heart, who is there? Every single fucking time? Huh? Who is there to make you feel good again? To get you flowers? Make up a skit? Sing you a really bad song? Dance in my undies? Huh? Who is the one who does whatever it takes to make you smile again and forget that you even cared about them for five seconds? It's me. Me. Every. Single. Time. So, you bet your arse your shit decisions affect me! You think it doesn't break my heart every time you get treated like shit?"

The sensor light went out and Oakley awkwardly took a few steps on the spot. The light still didn't come on. He waved his arms above his head and still the dark sky remained. I pursed my lips together and bravely joined him by waving my arms around, too. The light still didn't come on. Luke jumped up and down.

Evie's frown slowly eased and she laughed in spite of herself.

"You look like a bunch of octopuses doing the Macarena. I'm going to bed. I'm tired and I'm shouting at my friends and that makes me sad."

She turned and headed back towards the house.

"We love you!" we all shouted together.

Evie laughed. "I love you, too," she instantly replied, without looking back.

And then the sensor light came back on.

The Eleventh Chapter

Cue music: Amy Shark, All Loved Up. The week that ensued was pretty chilled in our household. My phone buzzed every few hours to take my pills, followed within ten minutes by an SMS from Oakley checking that I had. He has never done that before. I've been having treatment for years and he's never kept tabs on it. Not sure why the new pills are different to him.

Evie and Luke passed each other as they got ready for work each morning, sometimes saying 'morning,' sometimes not. Evie ate tea in her room instead of on the couch with Luke and I.

Oakley only came around once because he was working double shifts at the restaurant.

I wrote in Gold Flecks every day, usually whilst laying on the trampoline. I read two books. I vomited, generally as soon as I woke up in the morning. I sang 'Zit Remedy is Here' more times than I care to admit. I baked a cake and ate a packet of FADS. I napped. I had a blood test. I did some grocery shopping with Mum. I watched a YouTube tutorial and tried to teach myself to knit.

I went through my wardrobe and tried on my old clothes; clothes that belonged to my old self, pre-cancer. It was strange being reunited with my blue floral skirt and the black lace top I used to pair it with, seeing my olive-green jumpsuit, my Camilla-wannabe maxi and of course, my red dress. Strange as in I didn't feel sad, like I perhaps should have. I felt excited. Like I was still there, the real me. Waiting.

I found my old favourite denim shorts and hurriedly stepped out of my trackies before I changed my mind. They were much looser than the last time I wore them but a belt soon fixed that. I picked up a t-shirt ironically embossed with the phrase 'Ain't Life Grand'. I ran my fingers across the lettering, wondering about the last time I wore it. I must have been still at uni then.

I wondered what exactly constitutes a 'grand' life. Was life only grand back then, when I had already beat childhood cancer, and lived each day since oblivious to the fact that the adulthood edition was getting ready to stake its claim on my life as I knew it? Does the fact that I am dying of cancer negate the possibility of my life being considered grand? I was likely sick for up to a year before my diagnosis and during that year I had my first kiss, I graduated university, I loved life. Even when I was tired. Even when I had ultrasounds and blood tests and bone density scans to find out what was going on; I still loved my life. It was grand.

And damn it, it is still grand.

"Fuck it," I said out loud.

I pulled off my slack t-shirt and replaced it with the fitted top. My mirror approved. I took in the sight of myself and agreed that "Yes, life is grand," and went out to the kitchen to enjoy my breakfast while Amy Shark's song faded into the background.

Throughout the whole week, Luke and Evie seemed to exist on autopilot. They went through each day almost robotically, without any feeling or enjoyment behind it. There was an air of uncertainty, an underlying tension, waiting to surface.

And then it did.

"Morning, ladies," Luke announced as he popped his toast on. "Thank God it's Friday, hey?"

Evie looked up from her cereal. Her spoon was just about to enter her mouth and she held it mid-air.

"Morning. You're awfully chirpy this morning. Did you forget that we're all in bad moods this week and not really speaking to each other?"

"Nope, haven't forgotten. Just fishing around for a bit of a truce."

He got the vegemite ready on his knife and waited for his toast to pop. "Because if it's alright with everyone, I'd like to bring Annabelle round for tea tonight."

Evie dropped her spoon and it made a loud clang against her bowl. She shook her head and seemed embarrassed. "Sorry."

I gave Evie time to gather her thoughts.

"Wow, big move!" I announced, deliberately trying to sound excited. "Well done! Do you want us to stay or we can go out? I would love to meet her!"

Luke's toast popped and he smeared the vegemite from corner to corner.

"No, no, I want you to be here. For you both to be here. I mean, if that's alright. Oaks too, of course. I was hoping we could all sit out the back and have a barbie or something. Or just order pizza. I don't know, what do you think?"

He picked up his plate and carried it to the table.

Evie raised her eyebrows.

"Well, um, I mean, yeah, great. This is really great." She smiled an exaggerated, forced smile. "Great, it's great. Let's get pizza, so no one has to cook and I don't have to wash her dishes after."

I swallowed my smile in response to her passive-aggressive bitchiness.

"So, you're okay with this?" Luke asked nervously.

"Of course!" Evie responded in an overly upbeat voice. "Can't wait! Totes excited! But first, I must get to work! You both have yourselves a wonderful day and I will see you tonight for Annabelle hangs! Stoked for Annabelle hangs! Yay!"

She cringed at the sound of her own voice and went to her room to finish getting dressed for work.

"Well, that was scary," I spoke to my toast.

Luke chuckled. "Just when I think I've seen all her personalities..."

"I think her name was Pamela."

"Or Mary Lou."

"Possibly Tiffany?"

"Did she really say 'totes' and 'stoked'?"

"Don't forget 'hangs'."

We shared a laugh before Luke announced he had to go to work.

"I hope you don't mind me noticing or saying," he spoke as he placed his dishes in the sink, "but I like you in those clothes, Mack. You look like you."

"That's exactly the look I was going for," I beamed back at him.

Mum and Dad picked me up a bit later for my check in with Doctor Young. I paid attention as best I could but I just wanted to get home to clean. I'd decided that I was going to make a real effort tonight, for Luke. I wanted to hose down the outside table and chairs and put up some pretty bunting.

"What do you mean when you say 'plateau'?" Mum queried Doctor Young further.

"This is our hope for the new cells. The therapy reprograms the patient's own cells but because Mackenzie's cancer is so advanced, ideally, we are just looking to slow the progress down. Even if we could just extend her life by a few extra weeks."

I might actually put up some fairy lights and make a playlist! I need to make sure there's no washing hanging on the line when she comes, too.

"But there's no guarantee that they can even reprogram the cells they were able to get?" Dad pressed further.

Yep, definitely going to make a playlist. I have no idea what type of music Annabelle likes though. From what Evie told me about their brief encounter, Annabelle is a bit dull, a bit uptight. From what Luke told me, they only met for a few seconds and barely even spoke long enough for Evie to form an opinion. Evie obviously has a reciprocated bad attitude when it comes to Luke's love life, but her impression of people is usually spot on. Ironically. She is the best judge of character out of all of us, except when it comes to the people she lets in to her own life.

So, my task of compiling the perfect playlist for tonight is a rather tricky one. I get the feeling our obscure eighties and nineties favourites would be lost on Annabelle. I'm thinking Adele or John Mayer will be the main acts, which means my monthly data is about to go through the roof: I don't have one single Adele song on my playlist.

Mum and Dad dropped me home and I got straight into my spring clean. My alarm sounded, so I hastily downed my pills, answered Oakley's message, cranked up Michael Jackson's Dangerous album and set about scrubbing the kitchen, bathroom, toilet and laundry. I was exhausted but pushed through. I wanted to create a great night for my friends and I was fed up with cancer taking that ability away from me.

Oakley came around about lunch time with Subways and his overnight bag packed. His unit was getting an end of lease clean done and he couldn't move into his new place until Monday so he was crashing on the couch for a couple of nights. We ate our subs out on the back patio; I sat at the table and Oakley indulged in his natural preference to sit on the ground.

"I can't stop looking at you," he shyly smiled as he divided the Subway cookies between us. "Can we burn the trackies now?"

I giggled playfully. "No, it won't last. I just wanted to change the vibe this week. It's been tense, you know? It got to me. I feel the need to pretend all the bad stuff doesn't exist, just for a bit."

"Well, speaking of changing the vibe, there's something I kind of sort of want to tell you," he spoke between mouthfuls.

"You're scared about Evie hanging out with Annabelle, too?"

"Well, yeah, I am. Terrified would be a better word for it. But nah, it's about my rental. It won't exactly be ready on Monday."

"Oh no, did it fall through? Don't worry, I like looking for properties. We can go have a look at some next week. Evie and Luke won't mind you staying on the couch for a bit longer."

"No, I mean it won't be ready on Monday because I'm not getting a new rental. I um, I bought a place."

My mouth dropped open in excitement.

"You bought a place? Oakley, that's fantastic news! Congratulations!"

"I've been saving up the deposit for a while now, hence working all those double shifts and I've been doing some catering on the side."

"Wow," I replied, shocked. "I didn't even realise you were looking to buy. That's fantastic. Seriously, well done. Where is the house? When do you get your keys?"

"It's not far from you, like a five-minute drive from here really. Greenacres. I pick the keys up on Tuesday, so I'll only need your couch an extra night. I think you'll really like the house, Mack; it's pretty old but I'm going to fix it up. And when I'm all settled, I'm going to the Animal Welfare League to get a dog. There's this old man, Bruce; he's been waiting six months to find his home. I've had my eye on him for a while now. He keeps popping up on my newsfeed. Everyone shares his profile but no one wants him. He's nine, really chilled. If he's still there when I'm settled, I'll get him."

Cue music: Roxette, Fading Like a Flower. I watched Oakley's face as he rambled on about the ceiling lights he was going to get installed and the bathroom renovations he had planned. He spoke as if he couldn't keep up with his own words; his facial expressions so blatantly portraying his enthusiasm and excitement. His words grew softer until his lips were moving without a voice and I could only hear Roxette. He seemed to be moving further away from me with each sentence, like a camera was slowly zooming him out.

The drums kicked off the fifty-four second mark and I found myself transported to a dream. We were opening the door to an old house. Oakley picked me up and carried me inside. We were painting the kitchen. We were shopping for homewares and I was appalled at his choice of dinner plates. We were deciding where to put the couch. We were unpacking groceries. We were putting the new doona cover on. We were playing fetch in the backyard with Bruce. We were brushing our teeth, sharing the same mirror. We were getting into bed. We were doing everyday life, together.

I was happy for him. I was. My heart wept but I was happy for him. I have wanted him to start his own life ever since mine began to end. I just didn't expect it to hurt this much.

Back in reality, Oakley's grin had spread even further across his face. Making plans really seemed to get him going. Setting up a future. Adopting his own little family and building a life. He looked so adorable and I was so disgustingly jealous, I cursed the universe. I wanted to jump down onto his lap, wrap my arms around him and say 'let's go get Bruce right now!' And I knew that he would kiss me and tell me he loved me and call me his Puppy Mama. But I couldn't be a part of his bathroom renovations. I couldn't argue with him about which light fittings to choose. I couldn't build a life with him because the one my body was desperately clinging to was very nearly over.

I think in this moment, I realised that I had been holding him back. He had been living his life on pause, because of me. For me even. He had been living in anticipation of me getting better. He assumed, or hoped, that I would become me again, me without cancer. He started working the double shifts when I was given the twelve-month deadline. I realise why now. He pressed play.

I can't possibly resent him for finally starting his life. He worked hard for his deposit. He can set himself up now like he could have done, should have done, years ago. I never realised that I was his anchor. I wish I could tell him how content it makes me feel knowing that he is going to be okay.

"I think you should contact them today, the Animal Welfare League I mean," I suggested softly. "Tell them that you want Bruce but you can't pick him up until Wednesday. Just in case someone comes for him or they give up on him and put him to sleep. I really think you should call them."

"Yeah?" Oakley's face brimmed with happiness. "Will you come with me when I pick him up?"

I pressed my lips together to stop my smile from escaping. Good God yes, I would absolutely love to pick up Bruce with you.

"I think it's something you should do on your own."

Oakley rubbed his hands on his knees and softly muttered, "Yeah."

He pulled his phone from his jeans pocket and googled the number.

"While you do that, I'm going to go tidy up the lounge."

I stood up, scrunched my Subway wrapper and headed into the house. I turned back to see Oakley with his mobile to his ear, waiting for them to answer. He was perving on my legs and I shot him a knowing look. He laughed and brought his hand up to cover his eyes.

Back in the house, I picked up the duster and allowed a few tears to fall as I set about making the T.V cabinet sparkle.

Oakley joined me a few minutes later and told me that he has a meet and greet with Bruce tomorrow. I hugged him and told him that I couldn't wait to meet him one day. He picked up the vacuum cleaner and started on the floors while I dusted every surface in the place.

My alarm sounded just as I finished wiping down the hallway table. Oakley looked up from the vacuum cleaner and raised his eyebrows.

"I'm going!" I teased, pretending to be annoyed. Oakley smiled and set about putting away all the cleaning equipment in the laundry.

We had the place looking amazing by the time Evie got home. We pinned fairy lights up on the patio and wiped down the table and chairs. Oakley mowed a lawn that isn't his, for a woman that couldn't be his, while she lay on the trampoline making a playlist of songs she didn't like, for a woman that probably wouldn't like her. I added a Shakespeare's Sister song at the one-hour mark for my own sanity; if the evening was going badly, You're History would give me hope that at least it was half way over. The overgrown grass surrendered to the excessively loud blades attacking them while I tried to find another hour's worth of Adele songs.

The playlist ended up stretching out for two hours and nine minutes. I was optimistically envisaging an early night, but also concerned that the absence of Spice Girls and the like might increase the likelihood that Evie will explode. She had a go at Luke for never bringing his girlfriends home or including them in our life: ironic considering she is the reason why.

I lit the vanilla scented candles I got for my birthday an hour before Luke was due to arrive home with Annabelle. I wanted the whole house to smell like vanilla. I was going to keep them for a special occasion but I guess for me, there is no better occasion than being alive.

Candles set an ambience that calms my soul. Ahead of potentially the most volatile evening outside of the original Melrose Place apartment block, now is definitely the time for calm.

Hey Gold Flecks,

Everything is ready for the unprecedented milestone ahead: hanging out with Luke's girlfriend. For the entire duration of our friendship, I have probably said less than ten words to all his girlfriends combined. It is only ever a fleeting visit, a passing hello, an awkward 'hi, how are you?' as I catch Luke hurrying them out the door.

So, this Annabelle girl, she has never met me before, never even seen me. Do you think Luke would have prepped her about me? Like, it's not normal for someone to wear a beanie all the time, and it's a bit telling to do so in the middle of the hot Adelaide summer. Mind you, even if it wasn't for the whole bald thing, a stranger can still tell that I'm sick. I am skinny, but not in an attractive way; in a bony, look like I will collapse any second kind of way. I don't know if it's in my head but I can always smell vomit lingering on my clothes and skin. I put so much perfume on but I can still smell it. Can anyone else? Can everyone else? My eyes are sunken. I am so pale. I have dry itchy patches on my arms. I have a permanent rash on my neck that makes me look like I haven't washed in decades. I look…sick. Will she know this already or will she be oblivious until she takes one look at me and inevitably wonders what the hell kind of drugs her boyfriend's roommate is on.

Actually, I don't know if I would prefer her to know or not before she meets me. Luke would have of course given her a run-down of his friends, but what would he say about me? "Oakley's really chilled, Evie's a bit intimidating, Mack has terminal cancer." Not Mack loves music. Mack is a bit shy and awkward but you'll really like her. Just "Mack has cancer," because that's who I am, all I am.

But then alternatively, if he hasn't told her, I will have to endure the curious stares, the pity glances, the nervous vibe. She will want to ask what is wrong with me but will fear being perceived as rude. There is no pleasing me; I hope he hasn't told her but I also hope he has.

I am struggling a lot with meeting someone new; you may be able to tell. When I pass people in the shops, it's cool; they don't know me, they are not going to know me, so their stares don't feel like a personal attack. They make me uncomfortable, but not in a personal way. But inviting someone new into my world is freaking me out. What if we actually become friends? Just one more person I am going to end up hurting when this is all over.

Oakley ran himself through the shower after he had finished the lawns and got dressed in a pair of black fitted jeans and a worn grey t-shirt. The image of him stepping out of the bathroom was worthy of an extreme close-up and my mind certainly did her best to do it justice. His hair has already grown long again. I zoomed in so much I could see the water droplets falling from his hair as he pushed it back of his beautiful face. Aesthetically, I'm not sure any other man could even parallel him. He is sweet to pretend not to notice how much I stare at him.

Me? I have pulled out every single dress I own. Every skirt. Every pair of shorts. I will look ridiculous no matter what I wear. It was so easy to fall into my trackie dacks rut because none of these clothes feel like me anymore, because I am not really me anymore.

I have a scab just under my chin that won't go away. It has been there for nine days but I haven't hated it as much as I do right now. I am contemplating trying to cut it off with scissors. I just want to pull my whole head off and throw it across the room. I am skin and bones but I feel fat and frumpy. I feel utterly ugly. Like seriously, I am disgusting. Gross. I stink like vomit. I know I do. It's all I can smell. It just oozes from my pores these days. My skin is awful. It's dry and it stinks like vomit. It doesn't even matter what I wear; everything will stink like vomit. I should just stay in my room and vomit instead of meeting a new person.

I'm going to wear my trackies tomorrow. I keep reminding myself of this. All I need to do is get through tonight. One night, Mack. Get through tonight and then you can get back to dying tomorrow.

The thirteenth chapter

My bed was covered in clothes. Every top, every skirt, every dress, my jeans, shorts, singlets, jackets (even though it is thirty-six degrees), and my black beret. I am wearing my white beanie to create some sort of psychological security whilst staring at a bunch of clothes that make me want to break down and cry. But my intention is to wear the black cap tonight.

Every piece of clothing represents who I used to be, who I want to be still. Staring at them strewn about on my bed does not create a wonderful feeling inside me.

Oakley sits by my dressing table, on the floor, with his knees brought up loosely against his chest. Watching.

"What's wrong with that floral jumpsuit thingy? That's perfect." I think he is feeling a bit over it.

"It's out of fashion by about ten years."

"So?"

"Well you need boobs anyway and mine have shrunk too much to be able to hold it up properly now."

I rubbed the silky material of the jumpsuit between my fingers. I liked this jumpsuit. Loved it actually.

"Let me choose?" Oakley's tone of voice was unexpectedly seductive for what the moment warranted and it sent tingles up my spine.

Cue music: Simply Red, If You Don't Know Me by Now. I turned my back on the pile of clothes to face Oakley. His head was playfully tilted to the side, adorned with a ridiculously sexy smirk. He studied my response: most accurately summarised as terror. I giggled and rolled my eyes at his cheekiness.

Oakley stood from the floor and leisurely moved towards me until his body was mere centimetres from my own. My god he smelled good. He brushed his hair off his forehead and wrapped one arm around my waist.

"Let me choose," he repeated.

His free hand traced delicately down my arm and then gently tugged at the hem of my singlet. He looped his fingers around the material and began to glide it up from my waist to my breasts. I gasped and he smiled. From the eager look in his eye, I could tell that he enjoyed making me gasp.

He pulled the top over my head, not taking his eyes off mine for a split second. He dropped the singlet to the floor and reached for a white lace top on the bed. He held it against my torso, wrapping the sides around my waist.

"Too big," he said to himself and proceeded to study the options laid out before him. I pressed my lips together as he flattened a floral blouse against my shape, smoothing the material against my chest and critiquing the fit. "Too big."

I watched shyly as he came back and forth to me, each time holding a different top against me and smoothing it against my body. I never really understood the difference between sexual and sensual, but standing here completely vulnerable, half naked, while Oakley pressed various fabrics against my skin, boy did I get it now.

My hands instinctively covered my miniscule breasts between each fitting, and his hands gently guided them to my sides whenever necessary. His torso hunched over as he stood in front of me, fiddling with the fit of yet another top, his head bowed low in concentration. The hands that he had just shooed to my sides reached for his hair, seemingly unbeknownst to me. I wrapped his curls around my fingers and unintentionally guided his head closer to my body. Oakley looked up at me with fire in his eyes and stood to his natural height, shifting our perspective. He licked his bottom lip and pushed his hair back off his face.

"Shall I push you closer to me, too?" He placed his hand on the small of my back and gently pushed me towards him. I breathed too deeply and he smiled at the noise.

My feet involuntarily stepped forward like they were told and I tilted my gaze up to meet his.

"I miss kissing you," Oakley whispered with a frown. His hands gripped onto my hips and my internal organs started to clench. I was desperate for his touch and yearned to feel his lips as much as I sensed he wanted to feel mine.

He inched his face closer and his warm breath tingled my skin. I told myself to turn away; if he did try to kiss me, remember how much more it will hurt him when I die; if he did try to kiss me, remember all those times I have led him on; if he did try to kiss me, remember I just can't give him the life he so deserves; if he did try to kiss me...

He did try to kiss me. His lips brushed so softly against my cheek that they barely even made contact, and then lingered there as if undecided about their next move. I closed my eyes, acknowledging their vicinity, and waited for them to find my own.

Seconds passed. I opened my eyes to see Oakley smoothing a red long-sleeved satin top against my torso. He nodded to himself and then picked up a black rah-rah skirt, ensured it measured against my waist, and then placed the two in my hand.

"I always love you in red," he spoke with a croak in his voice.

And then he left my room, quietly closing the door behind him.

"Stupid bitch," I muttered to myself, "what did you expect?"

The fourteenth chapter

Evie looked insanely hot, even for her. She teased her hair into a high ponytail and wore Daisy Duke style denim shorts paired with a man's white business shirt, rolled up to her elbows and tied at the waist. Her excessively large gold hoop ear rings, red lips and eyeliner flick made her look intimidatingly confident and I suspect that was exactly the look she was aiming for.

"Just missing stilettoes," Oakley muttered quietly while he read the New Weekly at the kitchen table.

Evie was pouring herself a glass of water at the sink.

"I don't need em. My legs are sexy as fuck anyway."

Oakley chuckled to himself. "Why do you even care? Who are you trying to impress? You don't want Luke, let someone else have him."

"Shut up!" Evie quickly snapped. "Sorry," she added just as quickly, sculling the rest of her water. "I'm not trying to impress anyone, okay? Except maybe myself. I just want to look hot. I don't know why, okay? I don't even get it myself. I just know that if I look good, I won't feel so shit."

She joined Oakley and I at the table.

"Why do I care? Tell me. Luke has been joking around about wanting me to be his for like fourteen, fifteen years. I've had my chance. I didn't take it because I didn't want it. So why am I feeling like this now?"

"Like what?" I asked. "What are you feeling now? Jealous?"

"I don't know. I just sort of took it for granted that he would always pay me attention first, over and above any dumb tart he hooked up with."

"To be fair," Oakley spoke with caution, "she's not a dumb tart. She's studying medicine at uni."

Evie glared at Oakley as he returned to the safety of the pages of the magazine. She took a deep breath, made some sort of 'omming' noise as if she was about to meditate and then snapped her head back like a woman possessed.

"Fuck! Enough!" she exclaimed. "I am done feeling this way! You are totally right. I don't want Luke, let her have him. But I still want to be hotter than her."

"You're hotter than everyone," I assured her.

"Scarier than everyone, too," Oakley whispered into the magazine.

Evie glared at him for the second time in five minutes.

The alarm on my phone sounded and I robotically reached for the capsule of pills standing in front of me on the table, just as we heard Luke's car pulling into the driveway.

Evie jumped out of her seat. "She's here! I mean Luke's home! I mean they're here!"

Oakley and I smirked at each other as Evie frantically rushed her glass over to the sink and straightened the tea towel dangling from the oven door handle.

"Do I look okay?" Evie smoothed out her blouse, uncharacteristically seeking reassurance.

"You look like a man's dream and a woman's nightmare," Oakley kindly replied as he switched on the back-patio light.

I downed the last of my pills and stood to join them in the middle of the kitchen, grabbing the waistband of my underpants through my skirt and yanking them up.

"This skirt keeps pushing my undies down."

The front door opened and the three of us stared at each other in silent anticipation. We listened as the door closed and Luke's muffled voice began to get closer.

"Maybe we should disperse, so that it doesn't look like she is walking in on a seance?" Oakley wisely suggested.

We each took a step back from each other and Evie took an extra step to the right. We looked like a boy band mid-choreography.

Luke turned into the kitchen, holding hands with Annabelle. She wore jeans with a sleeveless floral blouse and her shoulder length hair hang loose below a yellow scarf headband. If I had to choose one word to describe her, it would be 'pretty.'

I immediately looked to Evie who immediately looked to Oakley who immediately looked to me. Our triangle was stumped.

"I'll do the introductions, hey?" Luke awkwardly announced. "Annabelle, these are my friends. Well, family."

Oakley shook off our stupor and held out his hand to Annabelle. "Oakley. Nice to meet you finally."

I followed his lead. "Really nice to put a face to your name. I'm Mackenzie and this is my sister, Evie."

Evie smiled and clapped her hands together. "Who wants drinks?"

"A drink is exactly what I need," Annabelle laughed.

"Good," Evie replied, "I like you already."

Evie stayed in the kitchen organising drinks with Luke while Oakley and I showed Annabelle out to the back patio.

"I love fairy lights!" Her voice evidently went up an octave when she was excited. "Your home is awesome, such a cool space out here."

I smiled at her words and felt a surge of confidence. A compliment on my home was worth more to me than a compliment on myself.

Annabelle and I took a spot at the table and Oakley sat himself opposite us on the grass.

"Sorry," Annabelle quickly offered, "did you want to sit here? I'm happy to move."

"Don't worry about him, he always sits on the floor," I laughed. "Oakley is strange like that."

The moment of awkward silence that ensued was broken by Evie carrying out a tray with five glasses on it. Luke followed her, pushing the eski.

"We got beer, cruisers, coke, lemonade and your champagne, honey." Luke poured Annabelle a glass of champagne and she smiled adoringly.

"I'll be in that!" Evie poured herself a glass of champagne and sat next to our guest at the table.

Luke raised an eyebrow. "Since when do you drink champagne?"

"Since now. Since my new friend Annabelle here does."

Annabelle's face lit up. "Yay! I would love to be your friend."

The two clinked glasses and Evie proceeded to give Annabelle a rundown of what she usually drinks.

"But champagne seems so much classier than a beer," she laughed and Annabelle laughed with her.

Luke's eyes widened in shock at their chummy exchange, as did mine and Oakley's.

The conversation picked up at perfect pace. Everyone was chatting, swapping life stories, discussing goals and nibbling on Oakley's cheese and biscuit platter. I didn't say very much; mingling has never been my strong suit. I think because I was so sick in high school; I never had the opportunity to go to parties or out to the movies with friends or learn basic social confidence. I'm thirty years old now and sitting here makes me feel like a child, bored to be at the grown-up table, unsure of how to talk to anyone. Or relate to them.

Annabelle was a big chocolate lover. They met in line at Cocolat; Luke was getting his coffee in between meetings and Annabelle had just finished a lecture at uni. She ordered a large chocolate milkshake with extra chocolate.

"So, this voice behind me says, 'I have only ever met one other person who orders extra chocolate.' And I turn around, and there's this insanely hot guy smiling at me. So, I put my number in his phone straight away," Annabelle beamed.

Everyone chuckled and even Evie laughed, "Smooth!"

The door bell sounded and I have never been so relieved to hear the arrival of a pizza delivery guy in my life. I was socially and physically exhausted and welcomed the excuse to get out of there.

"I'll get it," I quickly jumped up.

I greeted the delivery dude and placed the five pizza boxes on the kitchen table. I sat down for a second, listening to the pleasant mingling outside. I was so lethargic it made me feel confused and I shook my head in an attempt to get my bearings and snap out of it. My chest felt like someone was sitting on it and my breath was laboured and struggling to make its way out of my body. I mustered the strength to stand, reminding myself that the pizzas would go cold and soggy if

I didn't take them out soon. Standing drained me of the miniscule ounce of energy I had left. I sat back down again before I fell. I rested my head on the table and silently cursed my body for not fighting harder.

The first tear fell just as Luke entered the kitchen.

"Mack! What's wrong?" he cried as he rushed up to the table. I lifted my head but it flopped forwards just as Luke caught it gently in his hands.

"I-I'm so tired," I managed to slur.

"Let's get you to bed."

Luke swivelled my chair to face him and picked me up with the same effort and strength it would have taken him to pick up a three-year-old.

"I got you, sis."

My head rested into his chest and my bottom lip quivered with emotion at hearing him call me his sister. He carried me into my room and laid me down on the bed. My eyes were too heavy to open and I tried to say thank you but the world seemed to be miles away from me now. I heard Luke's voice but couldn't make out the words. The door clicked closed and I stopped trying to stay awake.

When I did wake up, the room was in darkness. I stood out of bed and looked down at myself. I was wearing my flannelette PJ bottoms and 'I love Dylan' t-shirt. I didn't recall Luke changing me and my attire puzzled my thoughts. I walked over to my window and peered through the closed blinds. It was dark outside but I couldn't find my phone to see what time it was. I must have left it out in the kitchen.

Outside my room, the house was in darkness but I could see the light coming from the kitchen down the hallway.

I assumed Evie and Luke were asleep so I tiptoed my way down.

Approaching the kitchen, I became aware of the sound of Jimmy Barnes' voice, softly serenading the radio with Stone Cold. I stood against the hallway wall, peering into the kitchen doorway.

Evie's hand rested on Luke's lower back, his whole arm was draped across her shoulders, locking her in close to him. Their spare hands were locked together, seemingly ready to step into the tango. Their eyes were fixed on each other as their bodies swayed together to the music. Luke spoke the words as Jimmy Barnes sang them. Evie tipped her head back in laughter and Luke spun her around before she rested her head against his chest. Luke inhaled as if he was trying to absorb every piece of her aura. I smiled to myself and disappeared into the dark hallway, tiptoeing back to my room.

When I woke up, I instinctively reached for my vomit bowl. The bile forcefully pushed its way up my throat and out my mouth. My lungs ached.

I slipped my beanie on and opened my door, ready to take the bowl down to the bathroom. Evie's door began to open and I quickly pulled my door closed again, leaving it ajar just enough to see Luke carefully creeping out of her room.

The fifteenth chapter

Greetings Gold Flecks,

So, I'm in hospital today. Fluid has built up in my lungs so getting that sorted.

Seasons are changing. It's only twenty-three degrees today and it feels freezing. Finally, I can wear my track suit pants and not look like I'm in the wrong country.

It's only an overnight stay, and a problem I have had before so no fear of the unknown. Mum and Dad were here earlier after Oakley brought me in to emergency. He was showing me his house; he was only a few minutes into the grand tour when I collapsed in the middle of his amazingly big kitchen.

"That was the real selling point," he was telling me. "The agent showed me the kitchen and I was like, 'yep, life would be good here.' I could see myself cooking for my friends while Bruce waited at my feet."

And then I huddled over in pain.

Today is his moving day. We were all meant to be helping. I am fine here on my own, in fact I am really enjoying the rest. The bed is super comfy and I am watching a documentary on Scientology. Mum and Dad have stepped in to help Oakley move, almost in honour of me it feels. Luke took the day off to help and Evie is going after work.

Apparently after he put me to bed, Luke took the pizza boxes out to everyone and whispered to Oakley that he needed to go to my room. It was Oakley who had put me in my PJs. Luke told me that Oakley didn't come back out again until after Annabelle had gone home, two hours later. He helped

Evie and Luke clean up, took a pizza and went home. Luke asked him if I was still asleep and Oakley told him, 'yes, I stayed until I knew she was only going to sleep and nothing else.' Explains why I have ended up here; I felt pretty close to death that night. I must have looked it too for Oakley to sit on my bedroom floor for two hours.

Evie said she really liked Annabelle and the whole night was a massive success. She told me Annabelle excitedly blurted out "Oh! I love this song!" at the start of almost every track. She was proud to tell me that she didn't say one bitchy remark, not even when Annabelle drunkenly declared that it was her mission in life to go to Africa to help immunise children.

"Could she be any more cliched? Zero points for originality. So, she's beautiful and she's going to save the world. Steve Harvey will be so impressed."

Annabelle had asked if I was okay after I went missing for the rest of the night. Evie said, "I told her that you get pretty tired, pretty quick and were taking some new drugs to help you. She asked if you had cancer, and I said yes. 'You never hear of a horrible person getting cancer. It's always the nice ones,' that's what she said. So, she liked you, Mack. She thought you were nice."

It had been ages since I had met someone new and had to impress them or let them get to know me. We all have a light inside of us and I didn't know if mine shone bright enough anymore for someone new to pick up on it. I liked Annabelle, really. I told myself I wouldn't, only because I was expecting her to not like me first.

Luke drove Annabelle home and was back within half an hour, just as Oakley was leaving my room. I asked Evie if the rest of the night was fun, and she just replied, 'not really. We just cleaned up, saw Oaks off and went to bed.'

I let it rest.

Anyway, the nurse is here now to do some nurse stuff. She has brought me in a tin of Nesquik and a spoon. I love her. Once she is done poking and prodding me, I shall be back on my documentary binge.

Thanks for being there, Gold Flecks. Pisses me off that Dr Young was right about you.

The sixteenth chapter

We loaded our bags into the boot of Oakley's car.

"Just so you know, I'm really not a fan of you doing this." Oakley held my hand and pleaded with his eyes. "Don't let Evie boss you into doing it. If you don't want to, it's okay."

"Oh ssh, Oaks!" Evie replied with a giggle as she pushed her way through us and began to rearrange the way we had packed the boot. "I'm not bossing her into doing it. I boss her into most things, granted, but I would never make someone jump out of a plane if they didn't want to!"

We shut the boot and took our spots in the car. I rode shotgun and DJed from YouTube on my phone while Evie rode with Luke in the back. Luke was quiet today. Actually, he had been quiet since the morning I saw him sneaking out of Evie's bedroom. Neither one of them had said anything to me about that night, other than how they were both so happy with how well Annabelle had fit in to our group. As far as I can tell, she and Luke are still together. Just because I witnessed that beautifully intimate moment between Evie, Luke and Jimmy Barnes in the kitchen, and then spied Luke tiptoeing out of her bedroom, doesn't necessarily mean that anything actually happened between them. I guess.

Oakley rolled his eyes as I cranked up My Finest Hour from the Teen Witch soundtrack and sang along with passion to every line. Evie sang even louder than I did, grooving her shoulders with the attitude the song warranted. I saw Oakley smile at Luke in the rear-view mirror with a look of bemusement dominating his face.

"Well it's not as bad as last night's rendition of that Bugsy Malone song!" Luke replied to Oakley's look.

We had tea at Oakley's new house last night, with Old Man Bruce, as we call him. Oakley is right; there is something magical about him. He is a black Staffy with greying hairs around his eyes and mouth. He has arthritis and is really showing his age. He walks very slowly, preferring to spend most of his time chilling on the couch. The fact that Oakley loves him so much makes me love the both of them even more.

He suits Oakley. Some people are really in your face and demand attention. Oakley is quiet, always standing back, looking in. He observes everything but doesn't say much unless he is pushed to. He pauses before he speaks. He takes people's feelings seriously. He watches the world. Old Man Bruce was meant to be his dog.

We played Scattergories after Oakley's decadent Mexican fiesta. Oakley and I sat on his three-seater couch, divided in half by Old Man Bruce's cuddly bum as he snored his way through the first three rounds. Our animated argument over whether to accept Luke's answer of "solid" for a food in the S round finally awoke him for his slumber.

"I love him so much," I mused as he snuggled his big black head against my thigh, preparing for his second snooze.

Oakley ruffled the hair on the back of Bruce's neck. "You're alright, aren't you, old fella."

Evie held her phone up in front of her and snapped a photo in our direction. I smiled to myself and couldn't wait to see it but Oakley frowned and said "What's with the photo?" He seemed to be annoyed by it. Or surprised maybe. I don't think I will ever figure out how to decipher Oakley's repertoire of moody facial expressions.

"Family portrait," Evie smirked.

Oakley shifted uncomfortably in his seat. I looked down at my lap and smoothed out the wrinkles in my track suit pants. I wanted to see that photo so badly. I suddenly wished the evening would end just so that I could go home and pester Evie for her phone.

"Okay, losers, round four!" Evie picked up the alphabet dice and rolled a B. She flipped the hourglass timer upside down and the sand began to fall. "And go!"

First up was 'a fruit'. Of course, we were all going to say 'banana.' I spent way too long trying to decide whether butternut was a fruit or a vegetable and before I knew it the timer had almost ran out. Luke squealed like a child when Evie declared "time's almost up!", which made her chuckle. Oakley calmly rested his pen on his paper, finished before all of us as usual. I quickly jotted a few more answers down before Evie exclaimed, "alright dudes, let's have it."

Ironically everyone else had also tried to be clever this round, assuming we would all use 'banana' for the fruit. Luke put down 'brandy' and Evie ridiculously tried 'buttered strawberries.'

"You realise I'm going to make you try buttered strawberries, if you're going to insist they're a thing!" Luke laughed.

"They are! People eat them all the time in Melbourne!" Evie tried to educate us.

Luke sighed. "Panel says?"

Luke, Oakley and I all declared "not accepted" in unison.

Evie slumped back in her chair. "Whatever."

Oakley offered his answer of 'blueberries,' obviously wondering why we had made that question so unnecessarily hard on ourselves.

"Moving on, I put Braveheart for movies," Luke announced.

"Beaches," Oakley replied.

`"Would you like to put on a mud mask and talk about boys?" Luke teased.

"Oh, we're psycho-analysing our answers now are we? Careful dude, you classified alcohol as a fruit," Oakley confidently retorted.

"Bushfire Moon," Evie offered up her answer.

"Bugsy Malone," I finished off the round.

"Challenge!" Luke declared. "Bugsy Mawhatey?"

"Bugsy Malone!" Evie, Oakley and I cheered simultaneously.

"What or who the hell is Bugsy Malone?"

Evie and I jumped to our feet and burst into song. You Give a Little Love had never sounded so joyous. Oakley hopped in between us and draped his arms across our shoulders. We kicked our legs A Chorus Line style and swayed along with the beat we created.

Luke stood with his arms folded and stared at the crazy people in front of him, his face rampant with embarrassment on our behalf. "Um...."

We sang the entire song and committed Luke to a promise that he would watch Bugsy Malone with us next weekend.

We played another three rounds before the cancer adamantly reminded me who I was. My arms and legs began to ache, my eyelids felt dry and heavy and if I attempted to speak, vomit would surely come out of my mouth instead of words. Oakley helped me to the car and set me up in the back seat. Evie sat in the front while Luke drove. I slumped against the window and stared at the photo of Oakley and I on the couch with Bruce. I made sure Evie sent it to me the second we got in the car.

Safe in bed that night, listening to Luke creep down to Evie's room, I saved a million different edits of the photo. Different crops, different filters. We were both looking down at Old Man Bruce but Oakley seemed to be half-looking at me, too.

When we finally reached the field, the reality of what was about to happen hit me hard. For some reason I had envisaged a big huge jumbo jet; instead, I was greeted with a miniature plane that looked more like a child's toy, certainly not a machine strong enough to carry actual human beings into the actual air.

Luke and Oakley watched on as the instructors went through the safety procedure with Evie and I. They fiddled with our straps and ensured that our safety gear was properly affixed at least four times as they spoke. The vest thing felt heavy against my torso and it took more energy than I had reserved to walk with it on.

I robotically climbed up into the tiny piece of scrap metal. The noise of the engine was incredible and made me acutely aware of just how fragile my body was; I wondered if it was possible for noise to crush a person to death.

We took our seats against the side of the plane as the ruckus continued to slam into my ears and stress out my brain to the point of shutting down. The man whom I would be attached to on my descent back to earth, and thus ironically (given that I am dying anyway) responsible for my life said something and I smiled in response but the content of his words was completely lost on me.

The panic began to spread through my bloodstream and I could feel the hysteria rising through my body. The plane started to move along the runway and I instinctively screamed out, "OH FUCK!"

Evie bounced her knees up and down. She was actually enjoying this. She was so excited her bottom kept levitating off the seat. Her exaggerated smile almost made her look scary, delirious.

"Holy fuck, Mack! We're doing it! From our trampoline to the actual fucking sky! We. Are. Doing. It! Wooooooohoooooooooo!"

I tried to return her psychotic smile but catered to the more pressing need to tense my lips together to prevent from screaming. I literally sat on my hands, wedging them firmly underneath my thighs to stop myself from hijacking the plane and forcing them to abort take-off. Within seconds, the plane took its rough leap into the air, leaving my stomach perched on the runway, hoping I would come back and claim it.

"We're doing it, Mack! We're fucking doing it! We. Are. Doing it!"

Man, I wish she would stop saying that.

"We're doing it!"

Evie squealed like a teenager who had just ran into KJ Apa walking down the street. "We're doing it, Mack! We're living, Mack! Do you hear that, world? We are living! Take that, universe! Living!"

Evie had tears welling in her eyes. I swallowed down my selfish fears as the realisation of what this experience really meant for her smacked me right across the face. Every day, Evie lives with the fact that I am dying, just as much as I do. And she has done so since our trampoline days, just as I have. When we promised to jump out of a plane all those years ago, she was really trying to convince herself that I would make it to my thirtieth birthday. She concocted the most out-of-character experience for both of us, maybe as her way of cementing the fact that life is not planned, that we are not a mere diagnosis we must adhere to. Evie, the completely confident, in-control, perfectly put together, assertive, commanding woman. And Mackenzie, the nervous, awkward, always-plays-it-safe terminal cancer patient. Neither one the world would ever expect to jump out of a plane. Yet here we are. Touching the clouds.

Evie made a promise back on that trampoline, a promise to us both. A promise that we would still be sisters. Maybe even after I am gone. A promise that I wouldn't die a teenager. A promise that we would both become adults. A promise that we would live.

And that's what we were doing, right now. Right now, in this utterly, absolutely, ridiculously terrifying moment. We were living. And not just living to die. Not just getting through another week, tallying up a few more days before the inevitable. We were living to live. Back on that night on the trampoline, neither one of us truly believed that we would. But we are. I am. I am alive. And I need to start living.

"We're doing it, Eves," I nodded. "We're doing it."

My bottom lip quivered and I pushed my tongue into the roof of my mouth to stop myself from crying. I was so incredibly scared and I didn't know how I was going to do this for her, but I knew, dammit did I know, that I had to.

"Hey," I motioned to my sky-diving dude, "no matter what I say, no matter how much I try to convince you that I don't want to do it, no matter how much I refuse, make me jump. No matter what I say, I want to jump. Got it? Just force me. You jump. Even if I beg you not to. Jump. Make me jump, no matter what."

He had kind eyes and brought them to meet mine.

"No matter what," he smiled knowingly.

"I'm going first, Mack!" Evie shouted over the noise of the engine. "I want to see you as you come down! I need to see you coming down. Holy shit, man! We! Are! Doing! It!"

Yep, I got it. Please stop reminding me.

"We're doing it, Mack! Fuck yeah!"

My guy chuckled. "We're doing it!"

Evie laughed with so much joy it stripped the cancer of all its power and I smiled in spite of myself.

"We're doing it," I laughed along with them.

"This is it, guys," the pilot announced into his mouth piece. "First jumpers are good to go!"

I opened my mouth to let the breath I had been holding escape. Evie and her instructor stepped towards the other side of the plane and I was taken aback by the brutality of the wind as he slid the door open.

I watched in horror as Evie's feet dangled out of the open plane, literally just hanging in the atmosphere. The blood vessels in my eye balls practically burst as she abruptly disappeared into the sky.

"LIVIIIIIIIIIIIIIING!" The sound of her voice seeped into oblivion, taking any ounce of bravery I had along with it.

"We're up, no-matter-what-girl!"

My guy began clicking us together. I stared into space and smudged the sweat from my palms on my thighs. He worked roughly and kept talking about "don't forget..." and "whatever you do..." but the specifics were nonsense to me. My future entry in Gold Flecks would logically declare that I went into shock, but right here, right now, all I knew was that there was no way in hell that I was jumping out of this plane.

"Okay, we're going to move towards the door now, love," he shouted over the noise pollution around us.

My arms instinctively grabbed onto the back of the chair and I clutched onto the head rest with every ounce of strength I had.

"No matter what, Mackenzie! No matter what!"

"Fuck off!" I screamed hysterically. "Fuck off and leave me alone! Get away from me! Help! Somebody HELP ME! Get away from me!"

He pulled his torso back, no doubt intending to drag me back with him but I was physically stronger than either one of us expected. I could take on Hulk Hogan right now and there was no way I was letting go of that head rest.

"Mackenzie, no matter what! You need to do this! I have to make you do this! You told me! No matter what!"

"Get away from me!" I kicked my heel back and felt it connect with his shin.

"Fuck! I am so stressed here! You said no matter what! Do you want me to force you to jump? You're attached to me, remember? I jump, you jump!"

Under less extreme circumstances, I may have found humour in the poor man's exasperation.

"No matter what, come on, let's jump! Or not! Fuck, I don't know what you want me to do here! Do you still want me to make you? I don't know what you want me to do!"

"Please, I'm begging you, I don't want to jump! I've changed my mind! I'm begging you, just please get away from me!"

He threw his hands up in the air. "You said even if you begged! Fuck, do I make you jump?"

"No, please, no! I can't. I'm so sorry. Don't worry about what I said, you don't need to make me. Please, I just can't. I'll die."

The sound of the plane seemed to fade away and my guy, whose name I wish I had been able to remember over my hysteria, said the words that silenced my fears.

"But aren't you dying anyway?"

I loosened my grip on the head rest. Cue music; Russell Morris, Hush.

My heels scraped along the floor as the guy whose name I had decided would be Jeremy, for reasons unknown to me, continued to roughly guide our joined bodies to the vast space of air ready to swallow us whole. Have you heard this song before? Listen to it. Listen to it and tell me you can't picture a skinny, pale, hairless woman in the throes of hysteria, digging her heels into the floor while the young, fit, stressed and confused instructor behind her slowly pushes them towards an open door of an acual plane. In the soundtrack of my life so far, this has to be the most perfectly fitting song.

We reached the open door too quickly and I frantically stretched out my arms and clutched onto the sides for dear life. I began to sob uncontrollably, plead and scream and poor Jeremy just about cried along with me he was so confused.

"You can do this, Mackenzie. If you want me to make you jump, I will."

His words were loud in my ear and reigned victorious over the increasingly distant sound of the engine. It was just me, Jeremy and Russell Morris now.

"I have been doing this for five years and I would never in a million years jump with someone who wasn't ready or changed their mind. I could get into a lot of trouble for that. But for you, I will. If you want me to jump, with all your begging not to, I will."

I cranked up Hush as loud as it would go.

"YES!" I triumphantly yelled into the aggressive sky. "MAKE ME JUMP!"

Tears drenched my face and I mumbled "oh fuck!" between frantic screams of terror.

Jeremy edged us mere millimetres forwards, prying my hands from the door.

And then we fell. It was unexpectedly aggressive, like the last few seconds of bath water being sucked down the drain. I swallowed the air that was all around me as the abrupt force of the fall hit me hard. I screamed repeatedly into the sky, intermittently bellowing out a "fuuuuuck!"

We plummeted towards Earth, at a speed that I was certain would rip my face off. I screamed so hard my tongue vibrated against the force.

"Keep your eyes open! It's amazing!" Jeremy shouted over the pressure of the wind.

I opened my eyes and screamed louder than a human being should be able to scream. I woke up every sleeping person the entire world over.

"Close your eyes!" he laughed.

I instantly pushed my eyes closed tight and sobbed into the sky. I honestly felt as if every muscle, bone and molecule in my body was in the process of self-annihilation.

I sobbed, "I'm so scared!"

I heard Jeremy chuckle. My face was in agony. The fact that some people derive enjoyment out of this baffled me.

"Please make it stop! I'm so scared!"

The force of the fall was crushing me. We were falling, plummeting at a speed the human body was surely not built to withstand. Everything was so aggressively frantic and induced a rush of panic through my blood. I had no control over what was happening to me. I couldn't make it stop. It was such an unexpectedly familiar feeling and the grief of not being able to save myself came pouring out of me. I sobbed uncontrollably.

"You will like this bit better!" my human parasite shouted behind me.

Suddenly a jolt forced my eyes open and our bodies were forced to stand upright in the middle of the sky. The rush died down in a millisecond and a euphoric calm settled over us.

"We're sailing now, girl. Amazing isn't it? Look around you, take it in!"

The release of the parachute thrust my hysteria into slow motion and I couldn't hear Russell Morris anymore. We were descended in mid-air like a puppet on a string. I was absolutely terrified of heights. And beyond petrified of dying.

And in the last few minutes, I had faced them both. And I felt like I had won. I saved myself.

We floated, or sailed as Jeremy called it, through the atmosphere. The tiny world underneath my feet was beautiful. The wind against my face was divine. The aura around me was unparalleled. Here, in the middle of the goddamn sky, I felt safe. And alive.

"It's amazing, Jeremy."

"Lol my name's Corey, but yes, it is!"

My emotions came pouring out and tears of laughter washed my face. I blubbered right on top of Earth and could literally feel the wind wipe my tears dry.

Corey had his arm stretched out and I realised that he was filming us. I tilted my head like a confused dog and smiled out of sheer relief. I cried and cried.

"I love you, Evie! Please know that, forever."

Our slow descent continued and I took in the spectacular sight below me. Above me. Around me. I nodded and quietly reassured myself, "it's okay."

Is this what I will see after I am gone? Is this what the world will look like to me after the cancer finally evicts me from my own body? Will I have zoom capabilities, so I can pick a house and pinch my view to enlarge what is inside, who is inside? Will I be floating, sailing? For eternity? I looked around and wondered, and hoped.

"We're going to start coming in now," Jeremy shouted over the wind. I mean Corey. "You'll find we'll speed up a bit as we get closer. You've done brilliant. This has been the best jump I have ever done. I can't imagine anything topping this feeling!"

We both laughed and I frantically absorbed every angle of the view around me, attempting to familiarise myself with what could potentially be my every-day reality in a few more months.

The ground crept towards us. The tops of the trees signalled that we were home and I wasn't sure how I felt about that. We brushed past their leaves and I spied Evie waving her arms in the air like a mad woman, rushing towards us with a comically huge grin smothering her whole face. Luke and Oakley were running after her, cheering and clapping.

Our landing was more forceful than I had expected and I yelped as we slammed roughly onto the ground, collapsing into a sitting position. Corey unclicked us and I attempted to stand but my knees buckled and I fell, just as Evie caught hold of my torso and clutched at my body with all her might. It was a split-second moment, but it played in slow motion in my mind. She threw her whole body into the hug and her laughter echoed with pure joy.

"You did it, you fucking legend!" she laughed over and over again.

I was overwhelmed with emotion and could only cry into her shoulder. Luke and Oakley reached us and wrapped their arms around our embrace, jumping up and down and cheering hysterically.

"Did you shit yourself?" Luke laughed.

"YES! I very likely did!" I threw my head back and surrendered to the plethora of emotions that were running rampant through my body.

Mum and Dad rushed up towards us from across the field. Mum had her hands across her mouth and Dad was smiling from ear to ear.

"Your Mum was crying, she was bloody scared," Oakley whispered behind me. "Your Dad didn't take his eyes off you for a second. He didn't even blink."

Luke and Oakley stepped aside to give Mum and Dad room. They embraced us so tightly I even heard Evie whimper.

"Please don't ever do that again," Mum laughed and cried.

Evie and I rested our bodies in the safety of Mum and Dad's arms. There was so much love in that hug I'm surprised little cartoon love hearts weren't popping around us in the sky.

"We got the phone call on your way back down to Earth," Dad gently announced, seemingly out of nowhere and laden with hesitation in his voice. "Your cells are ready."

My head nodded against Dad's chest as I took in the meaning of his words. My cells were ready. I physically felt Evie nodding her head, too and her breathing seemed heavier now, but she didn't say anything.

My cells were ready.

It was almost as if I had left the planet and when I returned, hope was waiting for me.

My cells were ready.

"Oh," Mum perked up, "and why does Oakley's naked bottom keep popping up on my Facebook?"

The seventeenth chapter

"You don't have to help me pack, I'm okay to do it. Just takes me longer than you, that's all."

I sat on my bed, legs crossed, hugging my pillow, while Oakley fluffed around my room checking all my drawers and rearranging my dressing table.

"I don't want you to be in there, wishing you had something. The information booklet said it's better you don't have visitors, to minimise the risk of infection. I won't be able to bring you in anything if you realise you want it."

"You read the information booklet?" I smiled to myself.

"Many times." He robotically picked up my hairbrush from its spot in front of the dressing table mirror and went to place it in my bag, before stopping himself and looking at me sheepishly.

I giggled as he returned it to my dressing table, in slow motion for comedic effect.

"Mum rang before, she said she's seen memes of you now!"

"Christ sake, thanks for that, Mack." Oakley pushed the hair off his forehead. "A man can't even take a naked stroll around a hospital ward now without someone making it go viral. Least my butt looked good, as always," he winked.

I scrolled through my newsfeed to check the views tally. "Far out! You're up to twelve thousand views now!"

"Wonderful," he mumbled as he folded my fifth pair of tracksuit pants.

"You might end up getting a call from Ellen," I laughed wholeheartedly.

"Your laugh is worth it. I didn't realise you had so many damn pairs of trackies. I thought you just wore the same one or two. I've counted like 16 pairs, Mack."

"I need that many to keep up with my vomit regime," I smiled.

He ignored me. "I've packed them all, plus your creams, and a vanilla candle. You probably can't light it in there but you can still smell it, in case you miss home or something. And I bought you a spare charger. Your old one was looking frayed and it could shit itself altogether while you're in there and then you're stuck. Please don't let your phone die. Keep it charged."

He continued to organise my suitcase, determined to make Marie Kondo proud.

"I've put a whole heap of new songs on your MP3, Molly Ringwald DVDs are in the front pocket, but I'm keeping The Breakfast Club, bugger ya." His smile made my tummy flutter. "I bought you a whole heap of magazines and a serial killer puzzle book. They're under your bed socks, next to your notebook with the gold flecks on it."

He rolled up my last pair of track suit pants and squeezed them into the corner. I watched him critique his own packing skills and I pressed my bottom down into the mattress to stop myself from leaping onto his body.

"I'm going to miss you so much." The words escaped my mouth before I could think to censor myself.

"Fuck I'm going to miss you," he instantly replied, rushing to sit in front of me on the bed. "I'm going to message you every five seconds. You're my best friend, my true love and I would cut my arm off right now if it would make you better."

He spoke with such haste, all his words rolling into one, as if he had ten seconds to tell me everything he had ever wanted to say.

"I know what you live with, what you face, and I think you're a goddamn warrior. I don't care if this is ten percent on your side and ninety percent on mine. Whatever you need to make the fucked-up shit you deal with easier. I completely understand why you won't let me be your guy. I do. But just so you know, I am anyway. I am only yours. In any capacity you allow for yourself, and completely all in for me."

I searched my brain for a song but his words crippled me. Cue music; stumped. Just stumped.

"Can I tell you something?" I paused as I tried to get my speech right in my mind. "I was going to pack my hairbrush, too. In fact, I will. I'm going to pack my hair brush."

Oakley tensed his eyebrows and I could tell he was processing my words and mentally analysing them like he always does.

"I want to pack it. I need to pack it. I need to believe that even though I am terminal, even though I have maybe six months left now, that this new treatment isn't only for research. It's not only for them to fine tune and experiment and figure out. I need to believe that they still have hope for me, too. That's what my hairbrush is: my hope. It reminds me that no matter what, hope will always remain. Hair can grow back, terminal can become critical, critical can become serious. No matter how close to the end I get, I need to believe that I can still turn around. I need to believe that there is a never a point where there is no coming back. I know what it is at the end of this road, but you are at one end, too and I am fighting so hard to get back to you. You make me desperate to stay, frantic to fight."

Oakley stroked my hand with his rough fingers. "So," he hesitated, "I'm your hairbrush?"

My giggle broke the seriousness of the moment. "Yep. That cool?" I bit my lip and anxiously waited for his reply.

He held my gaze and rested his forehead against mine. I smiled at the vicinity of his lips. "I am going to brush your hair so fucking much one day."

My laughter filled the whole room. Oakley wrapped his hands around mine and brought them up to his heart.

"I love you, Mackenzie. So fucking much. I will be your hairbrush, your hairspray, your bobby pins, your beanie, anything else you need me to be. Got it?"

My God, I love you so much, too.

"Got it," I could only whisper.

Dear Gold Flecks,

Settling into my new quarters today. My nurses all wear special gowns and masks when they come into my room. Not a great feeling, really.

I did a quick Google on CAR T therapy, but the more I read the more optimistic I became, and strangely enough that's not a favourable emotion. I need to be accepting. Google toyed with the idea of remission. I can't allow myself to think about that. My hope, my hairbrush, is for more time. I know I can't get a lifetime, but whatever I can get that is more than I already have, I will take. Cancer has dominated my body for too long. Surely you can't come back from that. Surely you can't come back from terminal. Delete those sentences, take out 'surely.' I know you can't and I need to stop reading too much into the positive, glowing reports that come up when I google those four intimidating capital letters. I can have my hope, have my hairbrush because hope is not as crushing as expectation.

I wonder how they actually put the receptors onto my cells. Like that's pretty impressive hey. To re-engineer someone's own cells and then put them back into their body. Where do they get the things they add onto the cells? Do they whip them up in a mixing bowl? Do they 3D print them? Pretty bloody smart.

I wonder how the rest of the cells in my body will react when they are reunited with their old friends. Will they recognise them and be all like, 'hey girl, where you been?' Or will they be instantly suss of them? It's some real undercover cop shit when you think about it. Sending your own mutated cells into the war zone to befriend the enemy and trick them into thinking they are just like the rest, before unleashing their new found superpower.

CAR T clinical trials have shown remission rates of up to ninety four percent, even in severe forms of cancer. But Google left out some factors when it said 'severe;' is this like severe for 6 months, as opposed to severe for 6 years? Surely longevity would have a worsening effect on its success rate. Delete that. Take out 'surely.'

My room smells sterile. I feel so nauseous. I have fluids seeping into my arm and my next round of chemo scheduled to start in 2 hours. That will really help with my nausea...

I get my new cells on Friday. They call the process 'infusion.' I thought it was an operation, like they would have to cut my veins open and air-drop the cells straight in. But I'll be awake. It's just like getting my chemo apparently. I'll be able to wave to my cells on their way down the IV. Wish them luck as they head into battle. Take no prisoners, CAR T cells.

It's Monday today.

I don't even know what to write. I am so up and down. I am scared yet excited, or more specifically, I am scared because I am excited. They are not separate emotions. I am excited because I can't help but have hope, even though I can feel my body slipping out of my reach. And that tiny bit of hope makes me scared.

Sometimes I get a strange taste in my mouth, like a led, metallic taste. I have always wondered if it is my soul slowly working its way out my body. I read somewhere once that scientists theorise that our souls are magnetic. So maybe

I am indeed tasting mine, tasting my actual soul. The taste gets more prominent as the days pass and I feel that the more vivid the taste becomes, the closer my soul is to escaping my body.

My playlist mirrors my erratic mood today. I'm watching the bag slowly drip into my vein and I'm sure it's dropping in time to the currently playing Hey, Soul Sister by Train. An hour ago, the nurse was tapping her pen along to Feargal Sharkey's A Good Heart, and before that The Beatles' You've Really Got a Hold on Me got the cleaner disinfecting my sink with a sexy rhythm. I hope they all like working in my room. Even though they have to dress up like astronauts to enter.

Music has been on my mind a lot today. Well, funeral music, specifically. My funeral music. Everyone is meant to have a song, right? A song they play at the end. But my issue is that whatever song I choose, that song will be forever ruined. My family will never be able to hear it again without feeling sad. I love my music so much so why would I want to ruin one of my favourite songs? Solution: I've decided Toto's Africa will be played at my funeral, because it is my least favourite song of all time. A year from now, when Evie is driving home from work, Africa will come on the radio and she won't have to pull over and cry. She will laugh and say "Mack hated this song!" That's what I want.

The nurse is here now to connect my chemo. Good time for me to fade into a nap. Night, Gold Flecks.

Wednesday today. We just did a messenger video call, Oaks and I, and I tell you what, Gold Flecks: I have never missed the touch of a person more. I thought seeing him and talking to him would make me feel better, but it made me feel mega shit. I miss him more now than I did before our call, and my heart literally ached for him through the screen.

He kept me company for two hours. I showed him around my room. He propped up his phone on his fence so I could see him play fetch with Old Man Bruce and watch them run around the backyard together. His backyard is looking really good. He has planter boxes set up along the side fence and is half way through building a retaining wall across the back.

"Bruce thinks it's his own personal castle. He stands on top of the pile of bricks and supervises."

They are really happy together, Gold Flecks and it makes me glow that I get to see Oakley this way before I go. To see him set up. That's what I get to take away with me. I don't need to think about the years after I am gone; I tortured myself with that thinking. Life punched me hard in the stomach when it dawned on me that he would probably go on to marry someone one day. But I realise now, that won't be my Oakley. My Oakley ends with me. My Oakley will be running around the backyard with his dog, watching 80s movies and stealing my New Weekly magazine forever.

I'm having my second round of chemo for the week today. They're pumping it into me like water before I get my new cells. Well, my old new cells. I think I fall asleep like every three hours. Everything exhausts me, even talking or writing in you. Everything makes me want to take a nap.

Dr Young was here earlier, checking all my charts. She sat on my bed next to my 'chemo chair' and chatted about some show she started watching, Love is Blind or something like that. She thought it would be my kind of show. I didn't peg her as a reality dating show fan.

Hearing her talk about things I like made me drop my guard and without thinking I asked her if she had any children. I instantly felt rude and excused myself. Her body seemed to stiffen and she tensed up her facial muscles. But then she told me that she didn't have children and that she had had a hysterectomy when she was 19 because she had ovarian cancer. I was speechless. She informed me that that was what inspired her to become a doctor.

And then she just kept on talking, as if I was a friend, not a patient. She is 44 years old. She has been married for 7 years. She has 2 dogs and loves going to nurseries to buy new plants. She eats too much chocolate and loves trashy reality T.V.

I exhaled but it came out more like a 'ha.' Dr Young smiled at me and I smiled back, shock and confusion no doubt splashed across my face. "So that's who you are then, as an actual person," I marvelled.

"That's me, Mack. And I think I owe you that after all these years. You have been my patient for a long time. It's an honour being your doctor."

She put her delicate lady-like hands on mine and squeezed gently. "Get that chemo into you," she winked.

"What is your name?" the words escaped my mouth before I could retrieve them.

Dr Young smiled. "Miranda."

I watched her leave my room, closing the door behind her. My smile dropped instantly as I realised that her sudden desire to share personal information with me probably indicated that she knew I was getting close to the end.

Hey Gold Flecks,

My brand spanking new cells are being 'infused' at 4pm. I am having chemo at 10am and then in they go, Gold Flecks! I feel very peaceful.

It is 7am. I remember when I was sick the first time, back in my teenage years; if I was too sick to go to school, I would lay in bed and watch Mulligrubs, Bert Newton, Art Attack. I don't remember actually being stressed that I was missing out an entire year's curriculum.

Mum would hire a whole heap of weeklies from Video Ezy. Overboard, Harry and the Hendersons, Stepkids, Suburban Commando, Fatherhood...I remember them all. I remember how hopeful Mum was when she showed me the new batch every week. I remember the way she looked at me, desperation behind her eyes, waiting for me to express approval, gratitude, excitement, happiness...anything other than the misery that radiated from my aura. And I tried. I always tried. I tried to be overly excited, so grateful, even if I thought the movie looked boring and I had no desire to see it. I tried. It always felt that it wasn't enough.

She just wanted to make me happy. That's all she needed. To know, to see, that despite everything, she could still make me happy.

The main thing I have always struggled with about my cancer is the way it affects everyone else. In my first battle, I wasn't scared of dying because of death itself; I was scared because I didn't want to make my family sad, forever. When I started feeling too weak and could feel myself losing, I would mentally picture my Mum sitting on a pew in a church, crying, grieving. Dad put his arm across her shoulder and just let her cry. I would play the scene in my head every day. No soundtrack, just Mum's cries. That's enough to make anyone fight harder.

I couldn't stop vomiting one day. Mum called the home nurse and told me she was just going to check in on me. She promised me she wasn't going to touch me. I was in bed. My whole body ached as if it had just been attacked by a lion. My skin was stinging and underneath it felt like my bones were being rubbed against sand paper. My stomach felt like ants were eating the lining. The home nurse arrived and tried to push a pill up my bottom. I squeezed my legs together and screamed. And cried. And begged to die. She pushed harder to get it up. I was completely broken. Completely defeated. I didn't want to fight any more if this is what my days would be like. I had had enough. I was fourteen.

My Mum saw the home nurse out and then ran back into my room. She crouched over me and sobbed, uttering "I'm so sorry," over and over into my soaked green nightie. I looked into Mum's eyes and willed myself to fight harder.

I hated myself in that moment. I was selfish. I had wanted to give up, when she was the one who was watching me suffer, helplessly. I just had to lay there and take it; take the sickness, the pain. My family were the ones dealing with it.

So, bring on 4pm, Gold Flecks. The cells are going to kick butt when they get back in there. And I'm going to get a few extra months of this beautiful thing called life.

The nineteenth chapter

The nurse seemed rushed as she connected the end of the IV to the tap in my arm.

"This will take about three to four hours to flush through," she spoke to the IV instead of me. "If you want the bathroom, ring your bell."

She hastily picked up my chart from the table next to the IV pole and her pen aggressively jotted down some numbers. Her plastic blue booties crunched on the floor as she stepped back to the intravenous pole and tapped the bag twice with her pen. Her goggles were fogging up from her sweat and her gown had been tied up so roughly it kept slipping off her shoulder.

Her eyes narrowed and she spoke to the bag of blood, "need anything while I'm here?"

I looked over to the IV and saw the first drop of blood make its way down the tube. I quickly stared back to the door. "Have you ever seen Pretty in Pink?"

The nurse looked at me for the first time since entering my room and I could tell by the way that her eyes slanted that she was smiling under her mask.

"I have!" The tone of her voice changed to contain an element of excitement. "I used to watch it all the time!"

"Did you like the ending? Because there are some people who believe she should have ended up with Ducky."

"No way!" she laughed. "Just because he was obsessed with her doesn't mean she owes him anything. She loved Blane. The ending was perfect. And that kiss? So consuming she drops her purse! Oooh Lord, I remember it well!"

I chuckled as the nurse's spirits lifted. "Hope the rest of your shift goes okay."

She nodded and placed the call bell across my lap, on top of my heavy woollen blanket. "Ring it if you need me."

As she left the room, I stared straight ahead, scared to turn my head to look at the IV again. We were alone. A bag of my blood containing the spy cells and I. The bag that could potentially buy me some more time. I smoothed my hands down the front of my Pretty in Pink top, featuring my face photoshopped onto Andy's body. I loved the ending to Pretty in Pink. Apparently, some people actually walked out of the cinema when it premiered, angry that she didn't end up with Ducky. I think it ended just the way it should have.

I turned my head cautiously, just as another drop descended down the slippery dip. Maybe there is no such thing as a bad ending. Things end just as they are supposed to.

"Wow," I breathed. "Are you the ones who can save me?"

Another drop of blood fell the same time as a single tear fell from my eye.

Cue music: Rachel Platten, Better Place. If life was a movie, this would be my montage scene. My eyes followed each drop as it slid effortlessly through the IV, into my vein.

I opened the door and Oakley was standing there, holding a St Elmo's Fire DVD and a block of Top Deck. I lay on the trampoline as a teenager, laughing with Evie as she told me about the new boy that wanted to go out with her. Dad was getting in his car to go to work, dressed in his three-piece suit and he waved to me as I parked in the street. Another drop of blood fell.

Luke placed one of his infamous milkshakes in front of me at the table. He was the worst cook in the world but his milkshakes were something of a work of art. And he was always so chuffed with himself, maybe because he knew how much I loved them. He left for work and checked his hair in the mirror on the way out and I laughed. Mum sat at the end of my bed while I slept, stroking my legs and humming. Another drop of blood fell.

Oakley placed his Scrabble tiles on the board. Evie threw her head back, laughing ferociously at one of Luke's lame pirate jokes. The adoration poured from his eyes. Another drop of blood fell.

I organised the pad boxes and ticked them off box by box on the delivery sheet. I pushed my med trolley and administered my residents their morning pills. Another drop of blood fell.

Mum, Dad, Evie and I sat around the lounge room, talking; oblivious to the simple joy of being in the company of family. Old Man Bruce snored. Another drop of blood fell.

Oakley lay on the cement, reading a magazine while I hung out the washing. I looked back at him and he was already looking at me. I smiled shyly. Dad picked some bacon off Mum's slice of pizza and she playfully slapped his hand away. I lit a vanilla candle and breathed in my favourite scent. Another drop of blood fell.

Rachel Platten's voice faded out as the scenes blurred away and I sobbed.

"Please work," I blubbered to the bag of blood dangling alongside me, potentially controlling my fate. I rubbed the dandelion pendant on my necklace between my fingers. "Please work, just a little bit. I'm not ready."

The twentieth chapter

My bedroom smelled like vanilla candles and it brought warmth to my bones. My candle hadn't smelt the same in the hospital room. It was rendered powerless against the sterile aura of its environment.

It had been three weeks since I had seen my dressing table. I loved my fluffy white stool that sat in its middle. It had been three weeks since I had seen my New Kids on the Block poster, hanging faithfully on my wardrobe door. I had missed this room the same way I would miss an actual person. I revelled at the sight of the faded yellow paint on the walls, the artificial Kmart plants by my window with its chipped white plantation shutters. I took in the wonderful site of my sanded back bedside table; it cost me five dollars on Gumtree and instantly fit in with my eclectic space. I never realised how much I loved my room until this very moment.

Oakley held onto my waist. He walked behind me, almost holding me up and guided me to my bed. I am pretty weak and don't have the strength to walk more than a few steps without needing to rest.

I lay down and smiled at the scent of my sheets. Oakley pulled the covers up to my chin, tucking the blankets in under my shoulder line just as I like.

"Thank you, about time you took me to bed," I smiled in an exhausted daze.

Oakley raised his eyebrows and I wanted to pull him on top of me. Not that I had the strength to.

"Whatever they did to your cells, I like it. Get some sleep and then talk to me like that again tomorrow."

I giggled and he left my room just as Mum walked in.

"Thank you, Oakley," she politely spoke as they passed.

"I got her, Mum," he nodded.

Mum came and sat down on the bed. She stroked my head and started talking about Dad getting organised to take the car in for a service.

"And I'm a little worried that Evie is becoming obsessed with that Annabelle girl. She talks about her non-stop and even asked me if I thought Annabelle was prettier than her."

Mum always knows how to reinstate normality and make everything seem just as it should be. Mum's voice reasoned, "It's not healthy, I tell her" and then my eyes closed and I had the best sleep I have had in my entire life.

My room was dim when I woke up. I reached for my phone and was thankful to find it fully charged on my bedside table. It was eleven p.m.

My throat was dry and my mouth felt scratchy. I checked my beanie hadn't fallen off in my sleep and tiptoed out of my room to get a drink, holding onto the wall for strength.

The kitchen light was on and Evie and Luke's voices echoed down the hallway. I was excited to see them and felt my body gravitate quicker towards the sound of their conversation.

And then I stopped.

"You really think Mack would want that, Evie? How the fuck do you think that would make her feel if she knew that?"

I knew I should turn around and go back to my room, or else make a noise so they could hear me coming. I really wanted that drink. But instead I slipped into the darkness and stayed hidden against the wall, listening.

The silence of the night was almost scary and the pause in their conversation seemed to extend past what would be considered normal.

Evie finally spoke, and her voice sounded different. Broken.

"What am I meant to do, Luke? How do you think I feel, every single day, knowing that my baby sister is dying? Knowing that I get to live and do anything I want. To never have anything wrong with me, and yet everything is wrong with my sister."

"But that's not your fault, Evie and Mack would hate it if she knew."

I nearly asked "knew what?" before remembering myself.

"I don't expect you to understand. You don't have a brother or a sister."

"Incorrect. Mack is my sister, too."

Silence again.

"Okay, I get that. And I don't know how to explain it so that you'll understand."

"I don't understand, Evie, I don't at all. You admit you're in love with me but you won't be with me."

My mouth dropped open in the darkness.

"You let me creep into your room almost every night, just so we can talk and have some time together. You won't even let me kiss you, yet you admit you love me."

"I knew it was you the night of the formal, Luke." Evie's voice trembled and my heart broke with her words. "I knew that first night I met you, that I was meant to be with you. That's why I couldn't talk to you, wouldn't talk to you. Do you know how shitty it felt, to have met you, and known you were the one? I was seventeen and I knew my whole life. I knew who I wanted to be with, what I wanted to do when I left school, everything, I knew my whole life. So how is that fair? I have my whole life figured out, basically handed to me on a silver platter, and my sister is dying. I had no intention of even going to my formal! Mum said I had to because it would upset Mackenzie if I didn't go. And you know what, I could feel myself having fun that night and that is exactly what I didn't want. While my sister stayed at home yet again because she had fucking cancer, I was having fun and meeting the man I wanted to be with for the rest of my life. My sister was dying and I had my whole life planned out. It's not fair! I can't have this wonderful life handed to me while my sister just tries to survive one more day."

"You can't deny yourself a life because you don't know how much longer your sister is going to have one."

Evie's sobs induced my own. "Yes, actually. That's exactly what I need to do. She is my sister, Luke. I knew my whole life when I was seventeen and she didn't even know if she would make it to seventeen."

"She wants you to be happy," he spoke softly, and I imagined he was speaking into his chest.

"Yes." If Evie's words were written on paper, they would be rendered illegible by the smudges from her tears. "I know. But I don't want to be happy, Luke. I don't want to be happy while my sister lives like this."

I heard the back door close and knew that Evie had gone outside to cry on the trampoline.

"Fuck!" Luke whispered to himself.

His footsteps left the kitchen and headed towards me. I pushed myself back into the wall and slowed my breathing.

"Mack?" he whispered in shock as he reached me.

"I'm sorry," my words fumbled, "I just came to get a drink."

"I'll get you one, go back to bed."

I nodded and headed back to my room. I sat on the end of my bed and buried my head in my hands.

Luke entered my room and quietly closed the door behind him. He sat next to me on the bed and placed a glass of apple juice in my hands.

"You shouldn't have heard that, Mack. I'm sorry."

I chugged the apple juice in one mouthful. "I always worry that me dying is going to destroy my family," I whispered into my lap. "Turns out living is hurting them just as much."

I swallowed the lump in my throat. Luke guided my head to his chest and smothered me in his embrace. "I'm so sorry, Mack."

I let my tears flow and made a conscious effort to inhale the lingering smell of vanilla to calm myself down. "What do I do? How do I fix this?"

"It's just her way of coping, Mack. You can't fix it. It's just the way it needs to be." He spoke softly and sweetly and the tone of his voice reminded me yet again of what an inherently good person he is.

"But it would make me so happy to see Evie happy. I don't understand what she's saying. I don't want her to not have a life because of me, that's awful."

"Don't talk about it now, Mack. You need to be resting. The doctor said. Come on, back in bed."

I agreed that I needed to lay down. The tiny walk down to the kitchen had almost crippled me. My head rested on the pillow and I rolled my body to the side to alleviate the sick feeling in my stomach. Luke crouched on the floor alongside me.

"We need to fix this, Luke. We need to show her that this is not the way it needs to be." Energy swept through me and I was inspired to change the world, now that I was laying down. "I can't believe she loves you! This is amazing! I saw you creep into her room a few times and I thought maybe you were just hooking up! She actually loves you."

Luke chuckled and seemed to blush. He brushed my cheek with his sleeve.

"You didn't tell me you knew I was going into her room. Nah, we haven't even kissed. We just needed to talk; get through all the shit we have let build up over the years. Watched a couple of movies, made fun of each other's dating record. Which makes a hell of a lot more sense now that we have both thought about it. Some nights we fell asleep together but nothing ever happened."

"I will show her, Luke. I will show her that I need her to be happy, that I want her to be happy!" I envisaged Evie laying on the trampoline outside in the dark of the night. "I don't know how, but I will. Evie knowing her whole life back then when I first got sick doesn't make me sad."

"I know that, Mack, but it makes her sad."

I couldn't help but see the comparison between Oakley and I and I closed my eyes in empathy.

"I have to break up with Annabelle tomorrow and you need to rest. Get some sleep, and I will, too. You be okay?"

I nodded into my chest. Luke kissed my forehead and tiptoed down to his room.

"Fuck you, cancer!" I whispered into the night. "You really do ruin everything."

The twenty first chapter

"Slow down, old fella," Oakley called to Bruce. "He's really pulling today. He must be excited that you've come on his walkies."

I was trying to build up my fitness. I couldn't walk for longer than a few minutes without feeling worn out and I was determined to give my body all the energy it needed in order to be the best battle ground for my CAR T cells to wage their war.

I stayed in the hospital for two weeks after they were infused and the side effects have been minimal so far. Some patients apparently get a flu, but I feel okay. I don't feel any different but I don't feel any worse, except for maybe a slight hazy feeling in my head some days.

"I think I will be tired before he will be," I admitted, watching Old Man Bruce's wiggly bum lead the way.

"We can stop, do you want to stop? Let's stop."

I laughed at Oakley's panicked tone. "I'm okay, bit longer. I can do it."

Oakley tugged back on Bruce's lead and Bruce turned his head back to shoot an annoyed glance in his direction.

"He's stubborn like you," I laughed.

"Stubborn? You're a fine bloody one to talk, my Molly girl."

I had no words of defence. "True."

We reached a park bench and my body practically lunged towards it.

"I take it we're sitting now?" Oakley smiled as he sat himself next to me.

"Yep," I breathed slowly. "Need to rest for a bit. Will Bruce mind?"

"Nah, the old man loves to sit and watch the buses go by."

The O-Bahn track was busy at this hour, carrying all the city workers home at the end of their nine to five. We stared at the O-Bahn tracks in silence, enjoying the cool breeze as it reduced the surface temperature of my flushed cheeks.

I shivered and tucked my hands under my thighs.

"I'm not going to cope well with winter."

Oakley turned his head to face me. "It's twenty degrees, Mack," he laughed.

"Exactly. Winter."

He took one arm out of his jacket and stretched the brown leather across my back, so we were both warmed by its embrace. I smiled to myself.

"Pretty romantic gesture, huh?" Oakley looked at me with smooth eyes.

"You do alright," I mused as he rested his head on my shoulder.

A bus plastered in X-Men movie posters roared past. Bruce growled and looked back to Oakley for praise.

"How are you feeling about Friday?" Oakley spoke, ignoring Bruce's need for validation.

I breathed in deep enough to literally feel my lungs expand. "I'm pumped actually," I replied almost hesitantly. "I want to know how it is going. I want to know what is happening in my body because to be honest I feel a bit like an idiot that I can't feel anything."

"What do you mean?" he asked, frowning.

"Major things are happening in my body, like a war is raging. New soldiers have gone into battle. And I can't feel anything at all, about how it's going. It's my own body, and I don't know a thing about it anymore. I need a bunch of doctors and scientists to tell me, to tell me how I am. I'm hosting the war and I can't feel which side is winning."

Oakley nodded pensively. "Well it's sure as hell not going to be the enemy that wins any time soon."

I patted Bruce's back with my foot. "But you know that the enemy will win. You get that, right?" I swallowed hard. "If this can buy me a little bit more time, I can take that. I will be grateful for that. I don't want you to start hoping for something more. You will make it harder for yourself when the war is over."

Oakley shook his head adamantly. "I've been doing a lot of research on this, Mack. It's got a good chance. You need to believe it, too. Don't talk yourself into losing. Believe that it could actually fucking work."

"Why?" I cried, "so that it will hurt more when it doesn't? So that I get complacent and rely on false hope, and not feel the need to fight with every ounce of strength I have?" I pressed my cold lips together. "I need to believe that nothing is going to work, so that I keep trying as hard as I can to prove my fate wrong."

The cool evening air dried my eyes and Oakley studied them before committing to his words. "Okay. If that's your logic, believe it's not going to work. If that makes you fight harder, then I'll believe that, too."

The alarm on my phone sounded and I reached for the pills in my bag. I took a big sip from my water bottle and opened my mouth playfully for Oakley to see that the pills had gone down.

"Such a lady," he laughed.

"Oh, Mum and Dad are coming over for lunch tomorrow, do you want to come?" I smiled.

"I'm working at four. Got the dinner shift again. Thanks though. Nice for you to enjoy the time with your parents."

"You know, it really will be nice. I'm looking forward to it. Evie and Luke will both be out. Bit of a treat having Mum and Dad to myself."

"We better get you home then, my little fitness buff. The last thing you need is a cold."

Bruce led us back to the car and Oakley opened my door for me, as Bruce leapt in.

"Hey, back seat, buddy!" Oakley laughed. "Obviously I still need to teach my boy how to be a gentleman."

Bruce jumped through to the back seat as I chuckled and clicked my seat belt on. Oakley got in on his side and turned the keys to start the ignition.

"Mack," he whispered softly as he gripped the steering wheel, "keep telling yourself that it won't work, hey? Please? I need you to fucking fight."

"It won't work," I replied in an instant. "It won't work."

The twenty second chapter

"The girl was a nasty pasty, so I don't know if the orders will be correct."

Mum laid out the pizza boxes on the lounge room coffee table and opened the top one.

"Anchovies, that's your fathers," she announced as she handed Dad his pizza box. "Ours are the same, Mackenzie so take your pick."

I opened both lids. One of the pizzas had a few puffed-up lumps of cheese and it made me feel nauseous looking at it.

"This one's mine," I smiled, picking up the box with the smoother-cheese pizza in it.

I rested the pizza box on my legs and relished in the warmth on my trackies.

"Okay, here we go, what made the girl a nasty pasty in your eyes?" Dad asked mockingly.

"She was talking to the other girl there while she was taking my order. Treated me like I wasn't even there."

Dad winked at me as Mum mumbled, "little upstart, she was" to her slice of pizza.

The pizza warmed my insides and I was ready to devour my second slice within seconds.

"So," Mum seemed to speak almost apprehensively, "we wanted to have this lunch with you today, with just you. We asked Evie to head out with Luke for a couple of hours."

I instantly knew that something was wrong. But they couldn't legally go to one of my medical appointments without me, so I knew something was wrong with someone or something else. And that felt worse.

I bit into my pizza. "Everyone is okay, before you say anything else, right?"

"Everyone is fine," she nodded reassuringly.

"Everyone is fine," Dad reiterated.

We all took a bite of our pizza and waited for the next person to speak.

Mum took the lead. "It's done now, so I don't want you analysing it or reading anything into it and feeling anything other than happy about it."

"It was our decision," Dad went on, "it needed to be done, and we are not sad, Evie is not sad, we wanted to do it because we are your parents, and we are a family and we fight together."

The room seemed to be closing in on me. "What's happened?"

Mum looked at Dad and he nodded encouragingly.

"When Doctor Young told us that you were a compatible candidate for the new treatment, that was it. There was no way you were not going to receive it. No way in hell. Whatever it took, you were getting that treatment."

My eyes welled up and my throat became hoarse. "Did you have to do something? Did they need your kidney or something?"

Mum and Dad laughed. "What? No, you silly billy," Dad lovingly teased, "but they did need a lot of money for it. More money than we had."

I scanned their faces and read what they were afraid to tell me. "Did you sell the house?" I dropped my head and cried. "I'm so sorry."

Mum and Dad both rushed up to the couch where I sat and hugged me from all angles.

"Ssh," Mum whispered. "No sorrys, no tears. It had to be done, and we are okay. We have bought a little two-bedroom house just around the corner from here actually. Your father can still have his library. We didn't need a four-bedroom house anymore and the backyard was getting too much for us. It's okay. We're okay."

"But he won't have his shed. You won't have your patio. Our bedrooms. Our climbing tree." I cried so much that even my neck felt wet.

"There was no other way," Dad said firmly. "And if you think we wouldn't do absolutely anything to get you through this, you're just wrong. We didn't even think twice. We discussed it with Evie and she didn't hesitate either. You would have wanted us to do it if we needed the money for Evie, or for your mother or I. We are a family and we help each other, no matter what. A shed is just a shed. You are our daughter."

He hugged me tighter. "This is what counts. You are what counts. Our family is what counts. Nothing will jeopardise that."

I cried in Mum's arms. "I'm so sorry."

"We're not," Mum and Dad exclaimed in unison.

Mum laughed, almost exaggeratingly. "We got a fortune for it! We got you some lovely new cells and your father and I have our own little cottage!"

She was trying to make me feel better and it made me feel worse. My parents had lost their home because of me. My childhood was gone.

"I'm sorry," I whispered again.

Dad sang a Beatles lyric and I closed my eyes to concentrate on the sound of his voice.

I knew they were right; if Evie needed that amount of money or if Mum and Dad did, I would have told them to sell the house, too. But to be the reason why felt incredibly lousy. They had literally given up their home for me. The guilt swept through my body and I knew I would just have to live with this, for however much longer that would be.

"When are you moving?" I asked shyly.

Mum looked to Dad and I could tell there was more.

"We spent our first night at the new place last night. We moved everything last week when you were in hospital and we have cleared everything out. A developer was very keen to buy it and we got more than we were expecting."

I closed my eyes. "A developer."

"Yes," Dad spoke softly.

"Are they-" my throat croaked and I swallowed the words back down my throat.

"Yes," Mum gently answered. "They are knocking it down on Friday."

Silence swallowed the room and I rested my head against Mum's fluffy pink zip up cardigan. Dad sang another Beatles lyric and I smiled lovingly. Mum and I sang along to the next line, melancholy echoing in our voices.

We ate our pizza while Mum moaned about inevitably having to tell the Lawson's about their move. "You know they'll want to know how much we got for the house."

I bit into my pizza and sat quietly while Mum and Dad planned when they would catch up with the Lawsons.

I couldn't fight them on the truth: I would want them to do the same if it was for any one of us. But the guilt and shame won't go away. There are some things you just have to live with. Ironically.

The twenty third chapter

The week had started off pretty shit and the middle of it was turning out to be no better. Considering what was on the calendar for Friday, I guess the whole week was just a write-off anyway really.

The developer was knocking down my childhood home first thing Friday morning. I had an MRI and blood test booked for four pm.

I sat at the table with my milkshake and New Weekly magazine while Luke worked on his laptop opposite me. He was finalising the report for a case he had just closed.

My tummy gurgled and I laughed in embarrassment.

"Your tummy wants food, Mack. Remind it that Evie is on her way home with Indian for tea."

"Are you coming Friday morning?" I asked.

"Nah, that's something just you and Eves should do with your parents. Still can't believe you're actually going to watch them pull the house down. Not sure I would want to see it if it was me."

"I kind of don't want the house going through it alone, if you get me. I don't want to watch. But I feel like I have to."

Luke nodded as his fingers frantically glided over the keyboard. I could tell he wanted to finish the report before Evie got home with tea and I didn't want to be the reason why he didn't.

I gulped down the rest of my milkshake. "I'm going to have a shower, sing out if Evie gets home okay?"

"Okay, Mackie," Luke spoke, not taking his eyes off the screen.

The water from the shower was boiling and I relished the warmth as it stung my back. I smoothed the vanilla body wash over my limbs and rinsed the bubbles as the water cascaded onto my body.

I stood at the sink and began to dry myself; dabbing the towel over the discolouration on my neck and skimming gently over the bruises that covered the majority of my skin. I reached for the clean pair of trackies and jumper I had laid out on the edge of the bath and got dressed before I began to feel cold. I picked up my beanie as it rested on the stool and placed it on my head.

I stopped in my tracks at the sight of the stool and my mouth dropped open. I looked to the shower. And looked back at the stool. And then I looked in the mirror.

"My god," I smiled, admiring the person staring back at me. I had just had a shower, dried myself, and got dressed, all without feeling exhausted or nauseous. I had a shower standing up for the first time in maybe two years. I didn't even think to put the stool in. I got dried and dressed straight away, without needing to lay down naked on the bath mat, wishing someone else would come in and get me dry.

I sat on the stool as it stood idle in the corner and smiled the proudest smile I had felt worthy of in years. I was in awe of myself, and it was an incredible feeling.

The sound of Evie's car pulling up broke my self-admiration and I made my way out to the kitchen.

"Evie's home," I told Luke, just as he was packing away his laptop.

"Yep, I heard her car and I am all done! I'm ready to get my curry on!"

I made my way over to the cupboard to get the plates out and rested my hands on the sink for a quick second. I was starting to feel weak.

"I'll get them." Luke removed my hands from the sink and guided me over to the table. "Sit and rest, you've just had a shower, don't over-do it."

For a glorious few moments, I had forgotten myself.

Luke proceeded to lay the plates out on the table and get the cutlery out.

"Wassup bitches!" Evie bounced into the room, lifting both her arms out to the side, grasping a plastic bag in each hand. "I ordered so much food it didn't even fit in one bag!"

"I am genuinely starving!" I enthusiastically announced.

Evie took out the plastic containers from the bags and took the lids off each one as she presented them on the table.

"We got butter chicken, we got beef madris, we got biryani, we got tandoori chicken, we got chana masala, we got three flavours of Naan, we got papadums, we got food!"

"Are we going to be able to eat all this?" Luke laughed. "You know Oaks is working tonight so we've only got three mouths between us."

"I think we all know I can help out in that regard," I reminded them.

"Let's eat!" Evie joyfully declared as she took her spot next to me on the bench seat. "Who wants to tell me about their day? I'll go first. I had the worst meeting with our new Receptionist. I had to do her performance appraisal and it's pretty gut wrenching having to tell a sixty-year- old woman that she's not answering the phone properly."

We all feasted on the Indian banquet while Evie continued to blab on about every single detail of her day. She ate as if it was a race and spoke non-stop, until we were all full and our ears were sore from her voice.

"And that little twerp Damien better think again if he thinks he's going to succeed in his petition to move the accounts department to the third floor!"

There was a strange undertone to Evie's ramblings, like she was trying too hard or trying to compensate for something. For what though, I am not sure.

"I closed my case today," Luke cut in with an odd element of determination.

Evie looked down at her plate with its last remnants of butter chicken and nodded. She picked up a piece with her fork and put it in her mouth.

"Well since we're on to your life now, I got a message from Annabelle today," she suddenly announced.

Luke dropped his knife and I jumped as it clanged the plate.

"Oh?" His face went pale.

Evie cleared her throat. "She said you broke up with her. She just wanted to say it was nice meeting me." Evie looked at me and pressed her lips together. "She said she would be here for me when I needed her one day."

I knew what that meant and I smiled to let Evie know I understood.

"Why did you break up with her?" Evie studied Luke's face. "She was perfect for you. She was so nice. We all liked her. You finally get a girl who's not a frump and then you dump her. That was really stupid, Luke."

The tension in the air had built and I shifted uncomfortably in my seat.

Luke ripped off a piece of naan bread and abruptly stood from his chair.

"Guess I'm just stupid then." He stared down at Evie before walking away and slamming the door to his room.

Evie shook her head and put some more butter chicken in her mouth. "Idiot. She was perfect for him."

I wanted to tell her that I knew she had told Luke that she was in love with him. I wanted to tell her everything. That I wanted her to be happy. That she had got it wrong: denying herself happiness for my sake was just ridiculous. That she was the idiot here, not him. But I stared at my sister as she dug into some biryani and felt genuinely scared to speak. There was so much I wanted to say, so much I needed to say, but I couldn't.

I was terrified of making her erupt. Of making her mad at me. I am dying. I can't make her mad at me.

"Maybe…maybe it's a good opportunity for you and Luke to spend some time together." I stopped breathing and waited for her to scream at me.

Evie held her fork in front of her mouth. "Say what now?"

I exhaled slowly. "I just mean the universe is all about timing, you know?" I was so nervous the backs of my knees started sweating. "Maybe this is a good time for the two of you to try things out. I don't think there has ever been a time when you were both single."

"What the fuck, Mack?" Evie laughed and the sound was terrifying. "I'm not with Luke because I don't want to be, simple as that! It's got nothing to do with whether he has a new frigid girlfriend or not. Where did this even come from? I have no interest in Luke in that way whatsoever, so just shut the fuck up okay and mind your own business yeah?"

Her harsh words took me aback. "Yeah," I nodded and then just like Luke, I walked away and slammed the door to my room.

I sat on the edge of my bed and waited. Evie never lets someone else have the last word. She will come barging in any second to blast me.

Instead, there was a gentle tap on my door so I assumed it was Luke. "Come in."

Evie entered and I was shocked at her calm and seemingly sorry mood. "I didn't mean that. I'm sorry."

She sat down next to me on the bed. I was so relieved I wanted to cry.

"I was a bitch," she continued. "I shouldn't have told you to shut up and mind your own business. You don't deserve that."

Evie's eyes began to water. "I think I'm a bit messed up, Mack. I'm so angry at life, and so protective of you, and I don't know how to exist outside of that."

"Why can't you just let yourself be happy?" I pleaded with her.

"Because I'm not! And I can't be. How can I be happy, Mack when you're not?"

I frowned. "I'm dying, Evie, and I'm still happier than you."

I have seen Evie cry many times. But usually just over a loser boyfriend. This was different. So raw and cathartic. Evie cupped her face in her hands and sobbed years worth of tears right next to me on my bed. My heart broke and I wrapped my arms around her and cried too.

"You don't do me any justice by denying yourself a life, you know that right?" I summoned every ounce of bravery I had within me and kept talking. "It makes me sad, it makes my heart break and it makes me feel like you are dying along with me. I am begging you Evie, please stop refusing to live on my account. I don't want that, at all. I need the total opposite of that. I need you to have a life. I need you to stuff as much happiness and good times and experiences and life into your bones as possible. If not for yourself, for me."

Evie wiped her face across my jumper.

"Gross!" I laughed as I playfully pushed her away.

"You want me to be happy, hey?" Evie breathed as she dragged her sleeves across her cheeks.

"Of course I fucking do!"

Evie looked at me in surprise. "It always seems unnatural when you swear."

We both smiled and I chuckled to myself.

"Do you remember when we used to act out that Joanie and Chachi scene? The one where they broke up and Joanie said that she threw his sweater in the fire place?" I sighed lovingly. "You always made me be Chachi. And I just did whatever you told me, because you're my big sister and I absolutely adore you. But I'm telling you what to do for once, Evie. You are making a mistake. You are sabotaging something that doesn't need to be sabotaged. I'm telling you, Evie. I'm telling you. You are in love with Luke. You know it. So just be with him. Let yourself be happy."

Evie exhaled like she was having a contraction. "I tell you what, Mack. I'll let myself be happy when you do."

"I'm happy!" I laughed.

"Oh really?" she pressed on, sternly. "Why won't you be with Oakley then?"

"That's different, Eves. You know it."

"Actually, I don't know it, little sis. I don't see how it's different at all. You tell me to stop denying myself happiness yet that's exactly what you have done your whole life."

"My happiness will end up hurting people more in the end."

"Bullshit," she replied instantly. "That's bullshit. He loves you regardless, so he will hurt regardless. And in the meantime, you could be having a fucking great life instead of trying to convince me that I'm the only one who isn't."

I exhaled even louder than she had done seconds before. "I'm exhausted. I'm going to call it a night."

Evie bumped shoulders with me. "Night, little sis."

She reached the bedroom door and turned back to face me. "And I did let you be Joanie sometimes."

The twenty fourth chapter

It's Friday morning. 6 am. I didn't sleep very well, Gold Flecks. I don't think I have ever dreaded a day as much as I am dreading today.

Back in high school, on the days that I was well enough to go, I remember my stomach tying itself into knots as I walked in. Most of the girls stared at me. Some giggled amongst themselves. Some spat on me and called me a leper. Some moved away from me, even emptying out their desk and sitting on the other side of the room. I dreaded going to school. But I am dreading today more.

Back then I would lay on the stretcher bed for an hour, staring up at the ceiling while Mum held my toes and hummed to me. The nurse would be digging into my arm, trying to drain some blood from my collapsed veins. I dreaded getting those blood tests. But I am dreading today more.

Back in my university days, I would rush to the toilets after a lecture or seminar and hide in there until it was time for the next one. I had no idea how to socialise or make friends. I dreaded walking onto campus each day. But I am dreading today more.

Back when I would let my guard down for a few weeks with Oakley and then inevitably need to break up with him again, I would stay in my room for hours, just vomiting into my sick bowl. I told myself it was the cancer making me throw up. I dreaded every time I had to tell him I couldn't carry on seeing him. But I am dreading today more.

Today is the day my childhood home gets pulled down.

Dread is a weird emotion. It's not the same as scared or worried, or anxious even. It's like a feeling of fate almost. You know you have to do something. You know you have to experience it, no matter how painful it will be. Acceptance.

I am dreading today.

Our home will be pulled down. And I accept that.

I would support Mum and Dad's decision to sell the house if our roles were reversed and it had meant saving Evie's life. But I can't help thinking, if I had died the first time I got sick, none of this would be happening. Maybe I was meant to go back then. Maybe in a Sliding Doors reality I did, and our beautiful home filled with so many amazing memories doesn't have to be destroyed today.

Mum will cry. Howl most likely. And I will have to stand there knowing I am the cause behind her tears.

I know the logic, I understand the necessity, I accept that it was the only thing that Mum and Dad could do. And I am so grateful, with every fibre of my being. They didn't even hesitate and don't seem to regret their decision, in front of me anyway. But it pained them, of course it did. I know they are hurting, for me and because of me. And it is a crippling burden that I will just have to carry.

If the new cells achieve even a minor victory and my life is able to be extended by a few months, will that be worth it to them? I am going to die anyway, why not just leave things as they are, and as they will be, and not lose our family home? It is going to be the same outcome at the end for me anyway. Why not reduce the fatalities? Why not make it less shitty? We are losing the home Evie and I grew up in, the home Mum and Dad have lived in for thirty years, for what? For potentially a few extra months of my life, not even guaranteed. In the end they lose me and our family home, when they could just be losing me only.

My self-worth is at an all-time low, Gold Flecks. How many people walk around knowing the exact dollar figure their life is worth?

I have tried, yet again to talk to Evie about the crap going on in her head. She just needs to stop. I am the one dying, Gold Flecks. She can live, she can be happy. Why is she denying herself this? How can I make her see that I want her to be happy? No matter what I say, she just doesn't get it. It doesn't do me justice or anything like that. It doesn't make my cancer go away or feel any less fucked up. What do I need to say? What are the magic words that will fix the mess I have unintentionally made out of my sister's life?

What are the magic words that encompass everything I need to say to Mum and Dad? I'm sorry. I'm grateful. I'm sad. I love you. Thank you. I'm so sorry.

Absolutely everything feels like it is reaching boiling point. And I don't know how to fix any of it. I live to keep the peace and yet everything feels out of my control now. I need everyone to be happy and no one is. What can I say to fix all this?

In a lot of respects, I deny myself the joy of living, for fear of dying. Is this coping mechanism, this self-preservation contagious? I exist to keep everything calm on the surface, so it stays that way after I am gone. So regret doesn't linger. So nothing is unresolved. But it's all superficial. You can sweep dust under a rug but it's still there. And if you do that every time you sweep the house, just imagine how dirty it really is under there.

The twenty fifth chapter

Dad has brought champagne. He says we will raise our glass as she goes down.

She doesn't look like a home about to be bull dozed. She doesn't look run down or tired or neglected. She looks like a home, not a house. Because she is.

Evie holds my hand as we stand on the street, lovingly gazing at the home we learned to crawl in. Dad has his arm draped across Mum's shoulders.

"Cheers, old girl!" He raises his champagne glass in the air and skulls down a hefty mouthful.

"Thank you for a wonderful life," Mum utters through her tears.

Evie and I are silent. We stare at the white paint on the fence; chipped in places and yet seemingly just brushed on only yesterday, when we were roller skating up and down the drive way. Dad had made us stir the paint for what felt like hours to a twelve-year-old, but looking back now it was probably less than two minutes. Although maybe not; Dad did seem to make us stir it forever.

He always looked after the house as if he was looking after another child. He treated her with respect, and he nurtured her, always attending to her needs with love and gratitude. He told me once, 'if you look after your home, your home will look after you.'

We were brats really. We never helped and carried on when we were asked to. I see that now.

Dad asked me to help bring some rubbish around from the back once. He was filling up the trailer in the drive way, ready for a trip down to the tip. I cried as if he was punishing me and I was so hard done by because I wanted to play Jungle Jill on the computer, not help carry tree branches.

Dad made me carry just two things around, and then acted so proud of me. And then he let me go play on the computer. And then hours later, when the trailer was full, I so undeservedly got the prize of riding up the front with him, off to the tip.

We stopped for 'travellers': any drink and any chocolate I liked from the petrol station.

My God, they were good days.

Those days, this house, my God, we are just so bloody lucky to have had them.

I lay on the couch, unable to stop dry reaching. I had been vomiting all day, and all that was left to bring up was a putrid bile. Dad had been at work. As soon as he walked in the door, he rushed into the lounge and sat on the floor next to me, holding my hand. He said, 'I wish I knew what it feels like for you.' The white carpet where he sat was stained from our feet but it didn't look dirty. That was just the colour of it now. The cane couch I lay on was splitting at the sides but it hugged me in all the right places. I lay there, he sat there. In our home.

Evie was playing with some slime, even though Mum had asked her not to play with it inside. She threw it up high, meaning to catch it, but it got stuck on the dining room ceiling. It eventually fell down a few days later, after Dad climbed up the ladder and pried it off with the broom handle. The stain is still there. In our home.

So many moments and memories, all tucked away behind that white rendered exterior. They will not cease to exist as she is pulled down, but it will hurt. It will feel as if they are being taken away too.

A man in a high-vis jacket walks up to Mum and Dad and hands them a clip board of paperwork to sign. Dad removes his arm from Mum's shoulders and he commences signing the pages. Mum's tears sound heavier and Evie lets go of my hand and hugs her. I feel too ashamed to look at her.

I fixate on our home before me. She stands there so proud, no doubt beaming for all the happy times she has witnessed and been a part of, oblivious to the wrecking ball etching closer towards her.

The first collision is almost deafening and makes Mum sob harder into Evie's chest. She buries her head as if trying to block out what is happening.

Dad raises his glass in the air and starts making a trumpet noise, saluting her as she goes down.

My eyes well as her interior becomes more and more visible with every swing of the wrecking ball. I am overwhelmed with gratitude. She gave me the best memories of my life, and now she is giving me the opportunity to keep having one.

Mum's tears reign victorious in my head and I mentally record the noise to ensure I never take what I have for granted ever again.

I say 'I am dying' when what I should be saying is, 'I am still alive.' I have been living just to die. What an absolute waste of this magical life.

No more. I will not deny my happiness any longer.

The walls crumble as if giving me their strength. And by God, I'm going to use it.

The twenty sixth chapter

"Try to lay as still as possible," the nurse who is prettier than even Sam Frost instructs me. "I just can't get it."

She shakes her head as if annoyed with herself and takes a deep breath. "I've never missed one yet, but your veins just won't give it up for me!"

I giggle in spite of myself and stare up at the ceiling. She is perhaps the prettiest woman I have ever seen in real life. It must be an alien feeling for her to be rejected. Even if it is by my veins.

"They all usually struggle to get the blood, it's not just you," Mum kindly assures her as she stands at the end of the stretcher, massaging the soles of my feet.

She pricks me again but the vein withdraws. "Your veins are infuriating!" Sam Frost laughs.

I press my lips together as she tightens the band around my arm.

"Sorry," she winces in sympathy. "Shall we try the other arm again?"

"This is the arm that usually comes good in the end. They use the finest needle."

"I am too, but your veins hide. And when I finally get one, it collapses as soon as the needle goes in."

Sam Frost squints one eye closed and squats so she is level with the stretcher. She glares at my arm as if coming face to face with her high school bully.

"You can't defeat me!" She almost sounds like Gandalf.

"Your father wants his Chinese for tea," Mum begins to speak out of nowhere, "so don't let me forget to pick it up on my way home. I'm having my Szechuan chicken!" Her voice is perky and upbeat. "Goodness knows what I'll get for him!"

"I'll get you my pretty," Sam Frost threatens my veins, "and your blood, too!"

Mum tosses up between stir fry and hokkien noodles for Dad while the nurse carries on performing The Wizard of Oz to my veins. I laugh at the absurdity of the moment and attempt to ignore the deep stinging sensation as the needle passes through my skin again.

"Got you, you bitch!" Sam Frost gasps and quickly clarifies that she is addressing my vein as the bitch, not me.

"She was no match for you in the end," I smile.

Sam Frost lets out an evil laugh and I feel slightly awkward at her comedic relief. I feel childish, laying here getting my blood taken for the umpteenth time, while my Mum tries to distract me. Having a nurse who cracks jokes and entertains her patients, while I lay here thinking she is the prettiest girl in the world, just adds to the feeling that I am still fourteen years old inside, surrounded by adults whom I rely on to get me through my cancer. And maybe my life, too.

I look down at the tube that is nearly full. Sam Frost quickly attaches a new one and begins draining more blood into it.

"Two more to go! We got this!" she cheers.

Mum pats my feet. "We've always got this, bubs."

Mum starts telling Sam Frost how many years I have been sick; all the blood tests, scans, chemotherapy, and now stem cell therapy.

"Poor little thing, you've been through so much and you still have the happiest looking face!" Sam Frost sighs in sympathy as she keeps a close watch on my vein so it doesn't collapse while she is trying to fill the third tube.

"She has been through an awful lot," Mum agrees as she adjusts the legs of my track suit pants.

The thing with going through a lot, is just that: you go through it. I feel almost like a fraud as I lay here listening to Mum tell Sam Frost about how cruel life has been to me. Mum wipes away her tears and collects herself after yet another traumatic blood test. Sam Frost catches her breath as the third bile nears completion. The relief is rampant across her face. It was hard on both of them. Me? I just laid here. It hurt, but I just laid here. Mum and Sam Frost went through it. I just endured it. And I'm not so sure they're the same thing.

I have never been to one of my doctor's appointments on my own. I don't even really listen to what Doctor Young says, because Mum or Dad are always with me, and I don't want to hear it. I know they will listen and they will know what needs to be known. I've actually been rude to Doctor Young throughout the years. I don't even show her the courtesy of eye contact.

I have never had my blood taken without Mum holding my feet. I've never sat in one of my chemotherapy sessions without someone from my family there with me; reading a magazine, playing cards, watching YouTube.

Until the cell transplant. I was there on my own because I had to be for infection control purposes. The thing that could save me made me concentrate, listen, pay attention. I didn't just go through the motions, I didn't just lay there, I didn't just take my pill because my alarm went off. I was involved. It was happening to me, to my body, and I went through it.

Sam Frost pulls the third tube from the IV and removes the needle attached to it. It feels like it has pierced through to the other side of my arm and my stomach turns as she applies the tape over the cotton ball.

Cue music; East 17, It's Alright, and I swear Mum and Sam Frost can hear it too. The nurse places the three flasks of my blood on a metal tray and leaps into the middle of the surgery, dancing with elation that her perfect track record remains intact.

"I still got it!" she announces with an American twang, wobbling her knees and flapping her arms around without a care in the world about what she looks like.

Mum of course joins in and I roll my eyes and laugh at the same time. I wanted to get up and dance with them but I knew I would faint if I attempted to sit up too soon.

Mum and Sam Frost dance around the surgery, oozing uncensored joy for life and unbridled happiness. They can't even hear the music and yet they keep the beat as if it echoes all around them.

I need to dance more often. I need to celebrate these moments. I need to start going through these moments. Experiencing them, not just as if they are happening to a stranger, or a character. They are happening to me.

I watch my life unfold around me as if I am watching a movie. I compile the soundtrack, but am I really going to live my life as if it is written by fucking cancer? Maybe it's time to get a new script writer once and for all.

And just like that, I begin to tap my feet along to the music.

The twenty seventh chapter

I've had a good couple of weeks in terms of my health. I have a nagging headache but haven't vomited more than once a day. Up until today.

It is nearing four pm and I am only just now conjuring up the strength to get out of bed. I was vomiting most of the night into the early hours of the morning. My sides are aching and my skin is so dry I feel like it will flake off if anyone touches me.

At my appointment last week, Doctor Young told Mum that the effects of the chemotherapy would take months to leave my body, maybe even a couple of years. She told Mum because she is so accustomed to speaking to her and her alone, as opposed to the withdrawn brat typically slumped in the chair next to her.

"Can I stop taking the pills as well or is it just the intravenous chemo we are stopping?"

As if I had just announced that I was running off to the join the Church of Scientology, a stumped silence befell upon Mum and Doctor Young. Turning their heads in unison to face me, pride poured from Mum's eyes, and I imagined that this is what she would have looked like at my high school graduation ceremony, if I had been well enough to actually go. Or at my uni graduation, if I had been brave enough to actually go.

Doctor Young was so taken aback she leant forwards in her chair.

"Mackenzie," she cautiously addressed me, "um…"

She shook her head as if answering a question she had mentally asked herself.

"Um," she said again, laughing self-consciously, "sorry, I lost my train of thought."

I'm not sure how to decipher Doctor Young's response but I choose to interpret it as a nice one.

"We want to give the new cells time to work freely, without being under attack." Doctor Young had re-activated her Doctor mode. "I have charted a new regime for you, but it does not include any intravenous treatment. The pills will be a smaller dosage. Your blood work was promising, we saw only minimal growth of the cancer cells but we want to start seeing a decline and they are still reproducing at this stage."

I heard all this with my own ears. Because I was listening. I maintained eye contact with my doctor and I sat up straight in my chair and for the first time in a long time, I felt like a grown woman sitting at the adult table.

I sit on the edge of my bed for a few minutes and give the nausea time to subside. I have big plans today, words I need to put into action, and I can't do that while I stink like vomit. I press play on the cd player resting on my bedside table and smile as New Kids on the Block's Favourite Girl begins to work its magic. I listen to the song in its entirety, slowly breathing to suppress the nausea and to refuel my new-found ability to take on the world.

I take my time in the shower and reluctantly use my stool to save my depleted energy levels. It feels cold this evening and my body aches with the cool air as I sit on the bath mat drying myself. I wrap my towel under my arms and sprint back down to my room to the solace of my fifteen-dollar heater from Cheap as Chips.

The bars begin to glow and the heat hits my skin with urgent relief. I sit cross legged on my white fluffy rug and rub my vanilla scented moisturiser into my discoloured neck and bony arms, over my wobbly knees and scarred tummy. I inhale deeply and absorb my favourite scent, smiling as I take in the way it makes me feel.

I Google the weather on my phone: around sixteen degrees right now. Strewth. I'm going to need to invest in some Thermal Long Johns.

I look over to my faithful trackies waiting ever so loyally on my chair, but for the first time since I can remember, I don't feel comfort. I feel resentment.

Cue music; Sugababes, Stronger. I leave the warmth of the heater and rummage through the drawer on my desk to find a pair of scissors. I return to my little spot on the floor, track suit pants in one hand, scissors in the other. And I start to cut.

I thought it would make me cry. But God it feels good. Maybe because I know I have maybe twenty other pairs, but right now, literally cutting my metaphorical safety net into tiny squares, I am invincible.

I collect the squares of material into a pile, walk over to the bin by my door, and without hesitation, chuck them in.

"I don't need a cancer outfit," I assure myself out-loud.

I pull a pair of black jeans from my wardrobe and a cream jumper that slips off one shoulder. The jeans used to be a slim fit but I'm not sure they will fit me at all now. I hope they do. My planned outfit will match my fabulous new attitude perfectly.

To my amazement, the outfit does still fit me. The jeans are certainly not slim fit any more; I put on a belt to stop them from slipping off my bony hips and the legs are more 70s wide-leg on my scrawny pirate pegs. But it's still an outfit and I smile at the realisation that I like the idea of possibly going shopping to buy myself some new clothes.

I step into a pair of black ankle boots and slip on Mum's special black corduroy hat. The girl in the mirror looks just like somebody that I used to know.

I close my bedroom door behind me and start walking towards the life that has been waiting for me to claim it.

In the kitchen, Evie is popping the cork on a bottle of champagne.

"Wow," she nods in approval. "You look fucking fantastic!"

I bite my lip uncomfortably but then mentally punch myself. "Thank you, sis," I smile.

Oakley is pulling a tray of mini pizzas out of the oven.

"Fuck," he utters under his breath as he turns his back on his gourmet delicacies. He places his arm across his torso and bows.

"My lady." He smiles that smile that he reserves for me and me only. No one else will ever be gifted that special smile, I'm sure of this.

I giggle and courtesy in reply.

"Okay you two flirts," Evie laughs, "Mum and Dad are already out the back. Luke's been entertaining them for twenty minutes so he probably needs saving now."

Evie and I make our way out the laundry door. It is a sight to cherish: Mum and Dad huddled next to each other at the patio table like a couple of teenagers on their Saturday night date. Luke beams when he sees us coming and relieves Evie of the champagne bottle she is cradling under her arm.

"You'd think you'd take the six glasses I'm carrying instead," she snaps at him.

I rush to hug Mum and Dad and take my spot next to them. "You should see the mini pizzas, they look amazing! Everyone hungry?"

Luke half-smiles and I want to tell him to ignore her but I can only smile in return.

Right on cue, Oakley breaks the tension and arrives with two trays of mini gourmet pizzas.

"This is just the entrée, folks." He places the trays on the table, picks up one of the pizzas for himself and takes his seat on the floor beside us.

I was counting on this predictability. Ever since I overheard Evie and Luke in the kitchen. Ever since Evie told me that I wasn't happy. Ever since our home sacrificed itself to give me one more shot at a life. I have been planning this moment. Literally practising it. Rehearsing.

"You've outdone yourself, again, Oakley," Mum states approvingly.

"We should wine and dine here more often," Dad agrees. "Speaking of which, pass the champers!"

The mini pizzas are divine and without even thinking, I down three before catching myself. My nerves are starting to tickle inside and I take a sip of my champagne to suppress them.

I scripted this scene. Not an ugly disease that dictates everything I do; the clothes I wear, the choices I make, the happiness I permit for myself. I wrote this scene. Me, Mackenzie. And I'm the leading actress.

Action.

Life isn't like it is in the movies, and I have come to realise that this isn't such a bad thing after all. In Terms of Endearment, she dies. In Beaches, she dies. In Steal

Magnolias, she dies. Evie is one hundred percent right: I am not happy. Independent of the cancer, I am not happy. I live in a glass bubble, in preparation to die. I spend my days wishing that life could be like it is in the movies, I guess to make my sickness easier to deal with. But outside of a Brat Pack classic, the movies are just as shitty as real life: people die. Even main characters die. So why settle for a movie when you could have a fucking life?

Evie is telling everyone about the new "spunk rat" security guard at her work. "He's not in a band, I asked."

Luke squints his eyes and pensively stares across the backyard. The Director calls the start of the scene and gives me my cue. And I take it.

My movie is ready for its Time of My Life moment. I feel like I am auditioning for a role in my own life. But I decide if I get the part.

I smile stupidly to myself and almost laugh out loud at the absurdity of what I am about to do. I walk over to the CD player propped up inside the laundry window and put in the disc I pre-hid underneath it; 1980s Rock Classics. I skip to the tenth song and 1927's If I Could begins to play.

A montage of Oakley dominates my thoughts. I am seeing him for the first time again. He is in the kitchen at Solli's and looks annoyed as Edwina touches his arm. He kisses me on the couch and I pull away as soon as I hear Evie's car in the drive way. He goes straight home to hide his hurt. He is driving me to the beach and looks at me when he should be looking at the road in front of him. He is dancing around the lounge room, trying to make me laugh as he endeavours to copy Jeff's flip from Girls Just Want to Have Fun. He looks up at me from his usual spot on the floor and smiles that smile that no one else will ever receive.

The song is exactly two minutes and twenty-two seconds in. I have rehearsed this scene in my head for days, and for real in the privacy of my bedroom, and I am so scared I can actually feel my legs wobbling. I immediately diagnose myself with stage fright. I feel ridiculous, but ridiculous feels alive.

I walk over to Oakley as he sits on the cement and stretch out my arm to him. He frowns and takes my hand with uncertainty. Close up of his hand in mine.

The drums kick in at two minutes, thirty-five seconds. I pull his arm and yank him to his feet and rush my lips onto his. His passion instantly ignites and he kisses me faster and harder than I can kiss him. The camera is panning around us; circling our heated embrace. I'm sure someone has turned up the music even louder.

His hands hold onto my face; the familiarity of his touch and the hunger behind his kiss make me feel like I am Debra Winger in An Officer and a Gentleman. I am bald, skinny, patchy, scarred...and he makes me feel like a movie star. This man loves me.

A million miles away, I hear Evie cheering like Julia Roberts in the horse racing scene in Pretty Woman: "wup, wup, wup!"

My mouth forms a smile and Oakley's lips mirror mine in response.

"Well, this is new!" Mum whispers to Dad.

"Eight or nine years ago, maybe. Catch up, love," Dad knowingly teases. "It's about bloody time!" he shouts, raising his champagne glass.

I giggle and rest my head against Oakley's chest. He feels like home. The top three buttons of his white shirt are undone and the warmth of his skin against my cheek induces instant feelings of contentment.

The music fades softly into the background and Oakley's own singing voice softly takes over. He sings the last few lines of the song so that only I can hear; cementing it as my new all-time favourite.

I knew he'd get it.

The twenty eighth chapter

Evie robotically closes the front door behind her. She doesn't flinch when her keys drop to the floor, loudly announcing to the painfully quiet house that she is home. She vacantly stares into the lounge, her back resting against the door. A veil of pain falls over her traditionally immaculate face, now smudged and sunken.

Crouching down to pick up her keys, she collapses onto her knees as if offering herself as a sacrifice, and screams. Her voice is wrought with agony and the pitch is barely recognisable as human. She screams over and over again, bellowing into the empty house before her, and throws the keys violently across the room.

She sits, cradling her knees into her chest and slams her fist back into the door behind her.

Her cries echo into the silence. "Fuuuuuuuuuuuck!"

She kicks her feet about hysterically and frantically grabs at the floorboards as if expecting to rip out blades of grass.

"Fuck, fuck, fuck, FUCK!" Her voice chokes under the pressure of her tears. "I'm so sorry! I'm so sorry, I'm so sorry!"

Her sobs render her breathless and her body begins to compulsively dry heave.

"Oh my god, Mack, I'm so sorry, fuck I'm so sorry. I'm so sorry! Oh my god, my sister."

Evie slides her body onto the floor and rests her head on the dusty floorboards. It has been three weeks since she has done anything that even resembles house work.

"I love you so much, oh my god please, oh my god. Oh my god, oh my god please, oh my god. You can't be gone. You can't be gone. Oh my god. Oh my god."

Her eyes widen in terror and her words spill out hysterically. "Oh my god, oh my god. You can't be gone."

Luke's panicked voice resonates through the closed door. He tries to push it open but Evie's limp body blocks its path.

"I'm here, Evie. Move away from the door so I can come in. I'm here."

His voice croaks and he weeps into the door. "I'm here, Evie. I'm here. Just move so I can come in and we'll get through this fucking fucked up shit together. I'm here Evie, I'm here. Oh my god this can't be happening."

Luke presses his hands against the door to hold himself up and aggressively scrunches his mouth closed as if trapping a demon inside.

"Fuck this can't be happening. Evie, let me in okay? Let me in, please let me in. I need you."

Evie crawls away from the door and curls herself into a foetal position. Luke apprehensively pushes the door open and cups his hands over his mouth at the sight of Evie, rocking her body back and forth on the floor, defeated. His throat moans and his blood-shot eyes gush more tears.

Luke is the one who has it all together; he wears suits to work, he goes to a barber and knows what number hair cut he gets, he reads Nick Hornby. The sound of his voice as it is now, broken, gutted, lost, is unnatural.

"I'm here, Evie," he manages to splutter.

"My sister!" Evie clutches onto the floor and sobs into her chest. Luke lays himself behind her on the dusty floorboards, draping his arm and leg over her shaking body.

"I'm here, I'm here."

Evie holds onto his arm and weeps into his embrace.

"Luke, my sister!" she screams. "My god, my sister!"

Luke's lips quiver and he tightens his hold on Evie. He presses his head on her shoulder, his sobs matching her own. "I'm so sorry, Evie."

"This isn't real!" Evie wails, her words so evidently torturing her. "This can't be real! Oh my god. Mackenzie. Oh my god. This can't be real."

Luke presses his whole body into Evie. "I-I-I know." You can't save someone from drowning when you don't know how to swim yourself.

"My sister, Luke! I want my sister back." The words burn her mouth with their brutal finality.

Luke's body trembles and he can only whisper through his tears, "me too."

Evie's quivering voice resonates across the room. "I want my sister back! I want my sister back!"

Luke sobs into Evie's shoulder and he tightens his hold on her. "I know, I know," he cries.

"Oh my God, Mackenzie, I'm so sorry!" Evie howls.

I would pan the camera out here and slowly fade to black. But I have no control over the scenes anymore. I can't demand a rewrite. No 'take two'. I can't cue music. The end credits just roll.

The end. It's so irreversible. If you get behind on your electricity bill, you can go on a payment plan. If you gain ten kilos, you can go on a diet. If you miss an episode of your favourite show, you can find it online. You can do something about everything, except death. Death is the only thing in life that we just can't fix. It is completely, utterly, undeniably, irreversibly final. And that's why it terrifies me.

I imagine a scene like this, Gold Flecks. If I die, this is how it will be. Destroying. Ugly. Gutting. Shattering. Final. There will definitely need to be a sequel: the audience will want to see Evie happy, to see her persevere, overcome. She will carry the pain in her heart, but she will keep living. She will go to work. She will read books. She will watch movies. She will dine out. She will live, because she has to. And then one day, I pray, Gold Flecks, because she wants to.

I hated A League of Their Own when I first saw it, because I thought the ending was wrong. But I understand it now. Sometimes the supporting stars are the ones we really want to see succeed, the ones that deserve it, need it, more. People would want to see Evie happy; they would want to see her go on to thrive and live an amazing life with Luke. So, if this is how my movie has to end, I know my audience will cheer for Evie, the same as they cheered for Lori Petty.

But Gold Flecks, who's even to say that Evie is the supporting actress? Maybe she has been the main star all along. Maybe this is her movie, not mine.

I have thought about things a woman my age should never have to think about, planned for things I shouldn't have to plan for another sixty years, but this is not the end scene I want for my movie. I am trying, Gold Flecks. I literally speak to my cells; I give them pet names and pep talks. I'm still the scriptwriter here. Aren't I…?

The movie industry is tough and cancer is my biggest competitor. The bitch has written her own screenplay and I fight every day for mine to be read first.

Tomorrow, I will know which script got the Greenlight.

I had new bloods taken last week and Dr Young will have the latest data for me to try to understand. I have booked an Uber and told Mum and Dad that I need to go on my own. If the cancer cells are still reproducing at this stage in the game, my CAR-T cells have lost.

It's my script versus cancer's.

I know which ending I'd rather watch.

The twenty ninth chapter

The app tells me that my Uber has been successfully booked for pick up in one hour. I know it's really not worth mentioning, but I'm a bit bummed about the car: it's a blue Holden Sedan. Hardly movie worthy. I was hoping for a Dazed and Confused style ride; a black, late 1970s Ford Capri would do nicely.

"Why don't you just let me drive you?" Oakley playfully nudges my arm with his head.

He spent the night, in my bed, for everyone to know, and he doesn't seem to plan on leaving any time soon.

"You know it's like eleven o'clock, are you getting up at all today?" I laugh.

"Do you know how many years I have been waiting to sleep over? How many times I have wanted to be in this bed with you?" He brings the blankets up to his chin. "I ain't ever leaving. I'm going to wait here all day until you come back."

I sit on the edge of the bed and finish getting dressed. The smell of my vanilla body wash lingers on my skin and I inhale deeply. Cancer makes you take note of the little things.

"Mum and Dad will be here when I get home. If you want to hear how my fancy cells are doing, you might want to put a shirt on."

I know Mum and Dad are hurt that I want to go on my own today. But I just need to. I will only be able to face whatever happens if I experience it for myself. Not second hand. And if I have my emotional crutches with me, I will slip into old habits and rely on them to simply give me a memo after. I need to be independent, so I can get myself through.

"My alarm is going to go off in a minute to take my pills. I'm going to go put some toast on and get an orange juice. Do you want anything from the kitchen?"

Oakley smirks as he runs his hands along the top of the blankets. "I honestly don't feel like I will need anything else, ever again. I have everything that I want and need."

He sits up and slides his warm palm onto my neck, kissing my lips gently. I still feel shy and bite my lip nervously as he pulls away.

He rests his forehead against mine. "I love you, Mackenzie."

"I love you, Oakley," I reply without hesitation.

Oakley rushes his hand to his heart and flutters his eyes. I swat him on the arm and laugh as I head out to the kitchen to take my pills.

I rest my phone on the kitchen table, just as my alarm sounds.

"I already know," I announce with elation.

I open the fridge to see a milkshake waiting on the top shelf, standing behind a little piece of paper with the words 'For you, Sis' written in Luke's handwriting.

I have never seen Luke actually cook anything. Unless Evie makes pasta for tea, or Oakley caters, he always grabs take-away. I don't even think he knows how to boil noodles. But he makes the best milkshakes ever, and he knows I love them. The one thing that he can 'cook,' he makes often, for me. Love comes in many forms and people reveal theirs for you in many ways, if you pay attention.

I take my pills and delete the recurring alarm from my phone. I will remember to take them; I both assure and promise myself.

I stand at the kitchen sink and swallow my pills with a mouthful of frothy chocolate flavoured milkshake. When I make my own, it never tastes this good.

Looking out the kitchen window, I am ecstatic to spy Evie and Luke sitting on the trampoline. I suddenly feel fourteen again and duck so they don't see me. I giggle with glee and cautiously peer up from the bottom of the window.

Evie sits cross legged, with a stern look on her face. Luke is doodling his fingers along the surface of the trampoline, looking down into his lap.

When Evie came home from her high school formal, and told me all about the night, sitting on the trampoline in our dressing gowns, I thought my sister was the coolest person on the planet. She was my Kelly Taylor. She was always beautiful, fiercely confident, assertive and carried herself like a woman twice her age. She told me about the boy from Black Friars, who wanted to dance with her. Who spent all night ignoring his friends so he could get to know the hostile girl in the dark green Miss JM dress. She told me that he had "good hair," nonchalantly describing him as a mix between Steff and Blane, only she had "no intention of ever being someone's Andy."

Back then, I knew she was suppressing the squeals that any seventeen-year-old girl would naturally want to make in this moment. But like so much that was happening to me, I pretended it wasn't there. Evie merely skimmed over the details of this 'Luke boy,' instead insisting on hearing how I was feeling and if I had managed to keep my tea down. And I went along with it.

Luke says something and Evie replies in animated retaliation.

"Come on, sis," I desperately whisper to the window pane, "you can be happy, too."

They seem to be fighting. Luke just stares at the trampoline and lets Evie carry on, as he has always done. Her muffled voice tells me she is never going to lower her guard without a fight. Or without a push in the right direction.

So, if this really is Evie's movie, maybe I'm the Director.

I hastily grab my phone and search REO Speedwagon's Can't Fight This Feeling on YouTube. I turn the volume down and crawl to the laundry door. I hold my phone to my ear, waiting for the chorus. Just before it sounds, I turn the volume up as loud as it will go and burst out the door, standing on the patio with my phone held triumphantly high in the air.

Evie laughs and Luke shakes his head; I know he thinks I am slightly crazy but he really should be accustomed to this by now.

I channel my inner Lloyd Dobbler, holding the music up high so that it can be felt all around the entire scene. I nod encouragingly, urging Evie to just let go. I have cued the music. It's up to her now to follow the beat.

REO Speedwagon cannot be denied: Evie throws herself onto Luke's lap and wraps her legs around him. She holds his stupefied gaze and silently mouths, 'I love you.' Luke cups her face with his hands and passionately caresses her lips with his. Well done, REO Speedwagon.

I fist pump the air and run around the trampoline with my phone held high, cheering for my leading lady.

If this is how Steven Spielberg feels every time the scene works out the way he wanted it to, friggin sign me up.

I celebrate the thrill of life just like Sam Frost inspired me to do; I dance around the backyard completely void of inhibition, waving REO Speedwagon in the air. Evie and Luke smother each other in kisses and I doubt they are even aware that I am still in the scene.

I am, and I have no intention of calling 'Cut.'

The thirtieth chapter

I hate this room. How can a space so elegant, so architecturally stunning, evoke such powerful feelings of hatred?

This should be a celebrity's home, not a cancer clinic.

I feel like an imposter sitting here in the waiting room, on my own. Like a runaway teenager who freaks out every time a grown-up walks past, in case they notice that I am actually a child and shouldn't be without my Mummy. Like I will 'get in trouble' any moment.

My appointment time was exactly fifty-six minutes ago but I sit here still. I text Mum, Dad, Evie, Oakley and Luke that I haven't gone in yet, so they don't panic that my appointment was an hour ago and they still haven't heard from me.

I have never had to relay information to my family before. On the contrary, they are the ones who normally have to tell me what is going on. It is a massive responsibility. Cancer claims more than just the life of the body it occupies and I owe it to my people to get the facts right.

A middle-aged husband and wife leave Doctor Young's room. The wife holds a handkerchief up to her nose and her sobs echo cruelly against the marble tiles and vast ceiling. She is in enough pain as it is without the building publicly drawing attention to her suffering. I wonder which one of them is dying. Most people would guess the wife. But my bet is on the husband. He is the one providing comfort. Death is harder on the people who will be left behind.

"Mackenzie?" Doctor Young stands in her doorway with a warm smile on her face, as always. She looks really pretty today; her floral dress and cream cardigan is softer than her usual three-piece suit.

I follow her into her room and she closes the door behind us. And it's at this precise moment that I wish I had my Mum with me.

Her desk is massive; it dominates the room and creates an aura of intimidation. I am feeling conspicuously small and the desk mocks me for it.

I don't know why I thought I could do this on my own. Now I am the one who will have to tell my parents that I am not getting better. Throughout the years they have always heard it first-hand from Doctor Young and right now I realise how much easier that must be.

I take my seat and swallow a ball of vomit as it rises up my throat. My clothes are constricting my blood flow despite being two sizes too big. I push a breath up my face to cool my body temperature down. What I wouldn't give to be wearing my track suit pants.

"This is a really big deal, Mackenzie." Doctor Young takes a sip from the glass of water next to her. "I know how huge this is for you, to be here on your own."

I laugh awkwardly. "Well I'm thirty now, so I thought I better grow up a bit before I die."

My distasteful attempt at humour lingers in the air and I sit in my chair self-consciously while Doctor Young sifts through my notes.

I never noticed that she has a photo frame with a picture of her two dogs sitting on this monstrosity of a desk. And in the corner of the room behind her stands a hat stand, currently holding an umbrella, a black duffle coat and a handbag that could probably fit a sink inside of it. There is a floor-to-ceiling bookshelf to the left of me. Amongst the books, owl trinkets and framed certificates, hand-written letters are sticky taped to the shelves, dangling down as if tinsel on a Christmas tree. I will forever wonder now what they say, and who they are from: people she has saved, or from the family of people she couldn't.

"Your blood work was interesting."

I nod as if I know what that means. Doctor Young smiles and I feel more at ease.

"I have charted up a new regime for you. We are lowering the dosage again. There has been no new growth of the cancer cells."

Life is noisy. The world is hectic.

But it falls silent. And stops suddenly.

I forgot I was meant to be concentrating, listening, paying attention. I obviously misheard.

"Pardon me?" I ask apprehensively.

Doctor Young laughs sweetly. "I know."

She smiles, but not for me. Moments like this must be why she decided to become a Doctor.

"We will do another review in three weeks but for now, there has been no new growth."

Doctor Young continues to speak but I don't hear a word she says. I am fascinated by the arch of her lips as they move up and down spouting words I can't comprehend. All I know is that she said there has been no new growth. Didn't she?

Doctor Young is in the middle of a sentence.

"No new growth?" I blurt out. "At all? The cancer cells haven't reproduced? At all? Am I getting that right? Is that what you are saying?"

Doctor Young seems to suppress the unprofessional urge to squeal. "Yes, Mackenzie. That is exactly what I am saying. There has been no new growth."

She hands me my new prescription, and even I understand that the dosage she has written is considerably smaller than what it normally says.

"This is a good track to be on. Let's keep travelling along this one." Doctor Young joins her palms together and brings them up to her face. She taps her fingers, reminiscent of a gleeful mad scientist, and her eyes smile at me with a look that could almost be mistaken as love.

I wait for my Uber outside the building. In my state of shock, I frantically search for something to ground me. I take note of the people rushing past me, hurriedly making their way back to work at the end of their lunch breaks. I focus on the Mum's group having coffee across the street, dressed in active wear. Of the cars honking with impatience. It's real. The world still turns. Life is still happening. I'm not dreaming.

I had denied myself the luxury of being optimistic about today. At best, I had hoped to hear the word 'minimal,' just like last time. 'No new growth,' that's what she said. No new growth. 'No', 'new' and 'growth' in the same sentence. No new growth. Holy fuck.

I forgot to check what car I was waiting on. I take my phone from my pocket to check the status of my ride, just as a red Toyota Camry pulls up to the curb. I sit in the back seat and stare ahead in a stupor.

"Good day so far?" Aadesh asks conversationally.

I contemplate my answer. "Yeah," I nod knowingly, "probably the best one ever."

I can't believe I am about to say this, but for the final time, cue music. Choosing my last song ranks right up there with one of the hardest decisions of my life. The end song can make or break the entire movie. If the song isn't a perfect fit, the captivation isn't there. The thrill of victory, the desperation to win, the fight to overcome: the audience will only feel it if the song inspires them to. If The Best did not motivate Daniel son to kick Johnny's arse, would we have cheered as loud? What is St Elmo's Fire without Man in Motion? When Carly Simon lets all the rivers run in Working Girl, I feel like I finally made it too, Melanie Griffith. And not many people will get this, but when Happy Ending kicks in at the end of The Pirate Movie, I fair dinkum want to hug every single person I have ever met in my entire life.

Win in the End is an interesting one. When I listen to it solely in audio form, I don't feel the same as when I hear it in celebration of Michael J Fox shooting the winning goal, as himself, not the werewolf. Perfect example of a song and an ending needing one another in order to be fabulous.

My ending is fabulous now. As of today, it is fabulous. I just need the song to go with it.

What song could I possibly choose to represent the plethora of emotions running rampant through my body in this insanely perfect moment? What song could possibly capture the energy I feel, the zest, the unparalleled joy and sheer gratitude that makes me want to rip open the door of this Toyota Camry and sing and run and laugh and cry and jump and dance...and scream "no new growth" so the whole world can hear. What song could I possibly choose to say thank you to the universe?

But I don't have to choose it; without conscious thought, it just starts to play in my head.

Cue music; Irene Cara, The Dream.

I sit in the back of my Uber and willingly surrender myself to the music. I close my eyes as Irene Cara's seductive voice creeps over the instruments. It bothers me that no one else can hear this.

"Do you mind if I put some music on?" I ask Aadesh.

"I put radio on for you?"

"Actually, I've got my phone. I know just the right song."

Aadesh nods at me in the rear-view mirror and I YouTube the final song on the soundtrack of my life. I want the whole world to hear it, not just me.

Aadesh chuckles. "I like this song you play."

"So do I," I smile knowingly. "It's perfect, hey?"

I ask Aadesh to stop the car early, one street away from home. I have so much mad energy flowing through my veins and damn it, I want to make this scene bloody amazing.

"Good day, young lady," he calls out the window as I close the door behind me. "Enjoy your song."

I run down the street; skipping, jumping, singing and dancing as Irene Cara resonates throughout the whole neighbourhood. I rush past dogs and don't even stop to pat them. I am completely immersed in my unexpectedly perfect ending.

The cool wind on my face physically reminds me just how good it feels to be alive, and to live. I really do get it now: they are two totally different things. I laugh out loud as I hear Evie's muffled voice in my head: "liiiiiiiiiiviiiiiing!" The wind on my face is nowhere near as brutal as when I (forcibly) jumped out of that plane, but right now it sure feels just as good.

I near the corner of my street and see my house just ahead. My energy level is dropping but I am desperate to get home now and my legs quicken to a determined pace. I will never again have this unfathomably flawless moment. I have one chance to get it right. One take.

I burst through the front door and my body instinctively gravitates to the lounge room. It is exactly as I had scripted it: Evie, Luke, Oakley, Mum and Dad are waiting anxiously, lined up like Gridiron players ready for 'The Snap.'

Oakley shouts "she's here!" as if no one else could see me. I stop in the door way and inhale the aura of trepidation. Luke is clutching onto Evie's arm and she is biting her nails, something I have actually never seen her do. Luke self-consciously wipes his eye. I didn't see a tear but he would make sure he caught it before it fell.

Oakley runs his fingers through his hair and shifts nervously on the spot. Mum's fists are clenched together; visibly ready to tackle the bad news she must surely be accustomed to expect. Dad rests his hands protectively on her shoulders as he stands behind her, as if holding her back from attacking the air. I survey the room and mentally record every detail. I want to remember this moment for the rest of my life. I have one now.

The electric guitar solo sounds. I drop my arms to my side and release years worth of fear, panic and pain with three gloriously victorious words which I bellow into the ceiling.

"NO NEW GROWTH!"

My focus shoots straight to Mum. She cups her hands across her mouth and runs on the spot as if she is busting for a wee.

"Thank you, God," she whispers into her hands.

"Holy shit!" Evie breathes deeply. "Is this for real?"

All at once, five bodies come crashing into me. Evie throws her head back and screams, and then Mum screams, and then Luke and Oakley, and even Dad. We scream our throats hoarse while Irene Cara's high notes reign supreme.

We collectively roar, "No new growth!" as we stomp the floorboards raw and vibrate the walls with our ecstatic cheers and cathartic laughter.

Our voices fade out and Irene Cara plays on while we jump up and down in our huddle; in slow motion, naturally.

Cut.

Roll the credits now.

Our movie, my life; they both deserve a happy ending.

Fuck, don't we all.

Thank you for watching.